T0157588

THE LAST
REVOLT

THE LAST
REVOLT

EXECUTED BY
A CLANDESTINE LEAGUE
OF REBEL INSURRECTIONIST

JIM FEAZELL

iUniverse, Inc.
Bloomington

The Last Revolt

iUniverse books may be ordered through booksellers or by contacting:

iUniverse
1663 Liberty Drive
Bloomington, IN 47403
www.iuniverse.com
1-800-Authors (1-800-288-4677)

ISBN: 978-1-4759-3528-8 (sc)
ISBN: 978-1-4759-3527-1 (e)

Printed in the United States of America

iUniverse rev. date: 7/9/2012

For Sherry, Shane, Jody,
Christian and Catherine.

ACKNOWLEDGEMENTS

Grateful acknowledgment is made to Wikipedia encyclopedia for permission to use Dates, Places, Names and Excerpts under the *Creative Commons Attribution/ Share-Alike License* 3.0., and the GNU *free Documentation License* to authenticate the novel THE LAST REVOLT.

PROLOGUE

The fall evening was warm and still on September 24, 1874, while on a railroad sidetrack at New Braunfels, Texas, a short way from of San Antonio, sat a boxcar and Pullman car awaiting connection the next day with a northeast bound Union Pacific train. A gallant troop of thirty Union soldiers, guarding the boxcar, and considering the nice evening for the time of year, decided to bivouac in the adjoining field.

It was exactly 2 a.m. in the morning that no less than twenty-five former Missouri guerrilla bushwhacker's crept stealthy and systematically into the field of sleeping soldiers. The horrific gushing of blood glistened like cheap red wine in the bright moonlight as the guerrillas calling had so competently conditioned them to the ease of killing. Without the slightest bit of remorse, they vehemently sliced the throats of the sleeping soldiers with razor sharp Bowie-knifes. Only three soldiers awoke and elected, without conditions, the alternative of being shot. A few minutes later two more former Quantrill raiders backed a stolen locomotive with adjoining coal car up to the boxcar and locked onto it. All but two bushwhackers jumped into the Pullman car. The other two rode on the cattle-guard of the locomotive so as to handle the track switching implements.

After a short way south they switched onto the main track and backed up for about three miles, cautiously nearing the depot, where they backed onto another sidetrack and intercepted a boxcar holding the bushwhacker's horses. They locked onto the car and eased back onto the main track toward Uvalde where they switched onto a closed track and headed north. The closed track was blocked off with a stack of crossties and a sign stating "track closed" on them, which they moved and later replaced, after removing two sections of rails and ties behind the stack of crossties. They took up the crossties and put into the coal car to be used as fuel, and slid the four rails onto the Pullman car floor. They then camouflaged the ground to appear that the tracks had long hence been taken up. Due to the terrible ongoing depression in the U.S., the railway industry had over-expanded by some 20 million in loans and had to shutdown many less needed tracks. A total of five northbound tracks from Texas to Nevada had been closed. This first unused track would in five days take them to a point where there was a predestined hideout for the locomotive and the cars. They traveled northwest by Pecos and Roswell, then north by Santa Rosa and northwest by Farmington. Continuing northwest into Utah and bearing west to Payson. Skirting Camp Floyd Stagecoach Inn, and continued north to the east of the Great Salt Lake, they bypassed Ogden and Brigham City, bearing west by Tremonton and into Idaho bearing northwest to Shoshone where their track passed under the elevated railway of the Great Northern Flyer and north to Hailey, where they sidetracked to the old abandoned open-pit gold mine of Lucky Basin, and went onto a second sidetrack and into the old railroad switching yard where they put their train into the repair barn and minting facility of the mine. Twelve more men were there waiting for them with their own mounts and pack mules for all forty-two men. All of the men got busy outside taking up the track and crossties leading from the switch to inside the barn, They then put the tracks and crossties inside the barn with the train, and cleaned up any signs of their ever being a track there. They then closed, and removed the track switching implement, and replaced it with straight tracks.

On breaking the lock and entering the boxcar, they took the top off of three dozen wooden crates filled with canvas sacks of newly minted Union gold coins of all denominations, including two crates of five and ten thousand dollar Liberty Head ingots. There was somewhere in the neighborhood of four billion dollars in that boxcar on the way to the U.S. Treasury mint in Washington, D.C.

President Ulysses S. Grant with approval of Congress had ordered the gold bought, minted and engraved to make good the promissory paper notes and greenbacks in circulation that were backed by gold, plus some to keep the government running in the worst depression in the history of the U.S. He had bought the gold from a mine and minting facility near Del Rio, Texas, and had it minted, engraved and stamped with borrowed money from a conglomerate of U.S. and foreign banks. The U.S. government was broke due to war expenditures. Lincoln had left nothing in the coffers.

It had been mandatory that the box-car be side-tracked overnight awaiting pick-up by the mid-morning Union Pacific with its destination being Washington, D.C. The Treasurer should have been less careless in its confidential covertness. This was just the chance that the Clandestine

League of Rebel Insurrectionist had needed to further their chances of resurrecting the south from the clutches of President Grant and the Radical Republicans in Congress of their unjust means of administering rules of the post-war Reconstruction.

Chapter 1

At the end of the American Civil War, Missouri was severely embroiled in the jaws of a highly conflicting contingency. The conflict split the population into three bitterly opposed factions; anti-slavery Unionists, identified with the new Republican Party; the segregationist conservative Unionists identified with the Democratic Party; and pro-slavery, ex-Confederate secessionist, many of whom were also allied with the Democrats, especially the southern part of the party. Due to the issuance of President Lincoln's Emancipation Proclamation on January 1, 1863, the Republican Reconstruction Administration passed a new state constitution that freed Missouri's slaves. It excluded Confederates from voting, serving on juries, becoming corporate officers, or preaching from church pulpits. The atmosphere was volatile, with widespread clashes between individuals, and between armed gangs of veterans from both sides of the war.

Scores of men left from the Quantrill and Anderson guerrilla raiders, including Frank and Jesse James, Cole Younger and his brothers, John, Jim & Bob, Archie Clements, and Junior Dunbar, found it hard to readjust to the ways of peace in Missouri in the years following 1865.

The natural violence of the frontier seemed quaint after the terror of the war days, old feuds and section antagonisms bred before and during the war continued.

It was claimed that these men tried to lead a peaceful life, but refused to be driven from their homeland, or suffer the antipathy caused by the extreme reforms of Reconstruction, especially in Clay, Jackson, Ray and Cass Counties, in Missouri. Jesse's mother supported his determination, and warned him never to surrender to groups claiming to be law-enforcement officers. Some former Quantrill raiders had surrendered and then been taken from jails and hanged, although the war was over. The atmosphere generated by incidents such as that was conducive to a life of violence. Many returned Confederate soldiers and ex-guerrillas that had even tempers patiently accepted the rebuffs and harassments of the triumphant Redlegs, Home Guards, and Union militiamen. However, men of hot temper and headstrong dispositions felt that the dominant element of society was turned against them, and that a life of outlawry was justifiable. Jesse and Frank James rode along with the Younger brothers and others that turned to a life of crime, robbing banks and trains. Esau Jones, a long time friend of Frank, Jesse and Junior had long since drifted west and became a celebrated bounty hunter. Junior Dunbar continued to ride with Archie Clements and his men as guerrilla bushwhacker's and bank robbers.

Confederate Regiment Captain Franklin Dunbar, with only six of his men left standing had been captured during the third and final day of the Gettysburg campaign. When the advancing Union soldiers were closing in on Captain Frank and his few remaining rebels, he undauntedly ordered his men to lay down their guns and raise their hands, in hopes that they might survive a sure death. They were taken captive and shuffled north to a prisoner encampment where they remained a few weeks until the war officially ended. According to the December 1863 Amnesty Proclamation, all prisoners in the camp were offered pardons if they would sign an oath of allegiance and swear never again to take up arms against the Union. Upwards of one hundred unshaven, un-bathed, hungry, sick and wounded men filed by a table in front of an army tent that day, and vocally uttered the oath of allegiance. They signed or put their mark by their name on a list. They were then shown the way south. Franklin Dunbar was one of the lucky soldiers that were never wounded in four years of battle. His capture was near the end of the bloodiest campaign of the entire war. In three days the Gettysburg campaign took the lives of fifty thousand Union soldiers and a like amount of Confederates.

Frank and a few other soldiers left Gettysburg headed due west, walking and hitching rides on logging trains, before turning south and walking across Maryland at its narrowest point. In West Virginia a small number of men intersected the south branch of the Potomac and followed the river road southwest through Petersburg where they saw dead soldiers still laying in fields and among the trees from the final battle of the war. Petersburg was destroyed with buildings still smoldering. The rebels scrounged food in Petersburg and pilfered good boots from dead Yankees. Bathing in the river had become a way of life on their long and tiring journey. The men were from all different parts of Kentucky, Tennessee and Missouri. At a point where the Potomac dissipated, some of the men turned directly west, while others went south toward Kentucky while others scattered throughout Tennessee. Frank and some of the weary men had to completely cross Kentucky into Missouri. Living in Kansas City with a wife and son, Frank had also to completely cross Missouri. By the time they reached Richmond, Missouri the number of men had dwindled to six.

Frank's son was fifteen when Frank went to war. He was named after him and called Junior. Unknowing to Frank, Junior, at two weeks into his sixteenth year had joined with Captain "Bloody Bill" Anderson's band of guerrilla bushwhackers. After riding with him for awhile against Union Militia and Yankee sympathizers, at which time Anderson was killed, he then rode with Anderson's Lieutenant, Archie Clement, who took command and continued to fight the Union militia left to oversee the Reconstruction. They also harassed the Republican authorities who governed Missouri. Following the surrender of General Robert E. Lee's army in Virginia, Clement and his followers had continued to fight.

Since most of the bushwhackers, including some of Clements men, were ready to lay down their arms, and swear the oath of allegiance, which they had been offered the same as Confederate soldiers, they rode into Fort Osage at Lexington, Missouri under a flag of truce. Major Bacon Montgomery allowed the men to surrender their arms and take the oath. After most of the bushwhackers left, Clement and a handful of his loyal supporters, including Junior Dunbar, stayed under arms and went to the bar of the City Hotel for a drink.

Seeing his opportunity, Montgomery dispatched a few Union soldiers to apprehend Archie Clement, who was wanted on a warrant for the Liberty Bank robbery in

Liberty, Missouri, and stealing $58,000. The bank was owned and operated by former Union Militia officers.

As the soldiers approached the Hotel, Clement and his men drew their revolvers. Shooting their way outside, they mounted their horses and galloped up the street, only to be riddled with bullets by more of the soldiers detachment, who were waiting with rifles loaded. Riding in front, Archie Clement was shot from his horse. Severely wounded he was trying to cock his pistol with his teeth when two soldiers killed him. Two more of Archie's men lay dead in the street, as a chase ensued with guns blazing. Outside of town at a hard run, Junior Dunbar was shot from his horse and rolled down a bushy embankment into a dense cypress laden slough. Another three men were run down and killed, as two got away.

About this same time Junior's Dad was somewhere in Clay County scrupulously seeking his safest route home to Kansas City.

Madame La'fay Beauxdeen de Dunbar sat in the drawing room of the Dunbar home, which comprised one-third of the third floor in the Grand Hotel of South Kansas City. Two men, Jim Poole and Virgil Sawyer, who visited her were friends and associates of her son, Junior.

"Mam, it bereaves me greatly to be the bearer of such sorrowful news," said Virgil.

"Yes Mam, me too," added Jim.

"From what you've told me, there is still a chance he might be alive, don't you think?" asked she, as she wiped her eyes.

"Yes Mam, by all accounts he could be. We circled back later and searched everywhere. We couldn't even find his horse. I believe the Yankee militiamen may have taken him back to the Fort," said Jim.

"What's the last you've heard from Captain Frank?" asked Virgil.

She looked unknowingly at Virgil for a moment before she realized that Junior must have told them about his father joining the army.

"I had a letter a couple of months ago that he wrote from a prison camp up in Pennsylvania. I cried and thanked God he was in the prison camp. That was my first letter in quite some time. I hear they have been releasing prisoners from camps. He could be on his way home."

"I certainly do hope so Mam. When he gets home, have him to go over to Fort Osage and inquire about Junior," Virgil said. "It would be taking too big a chance for me and Jim to go near that place."

"Yes, he and I will both go," she said. "Y'all boys stay in touch."

"Yes Mam," they both uttered as they left.

Madame La'fay Beauxdeen de Dunbar was an exceptionally beautiful and well-proportioned woman in her mid-thirties. Being of south Louisiana Cajun ancestry, with olive complexion and sparkling green eyes, she conducted herself with an air of dignity and respectability. Her dark glistening hair when struck by the sunlight showed a brilliant red tint. She had worked for a little over four years as a non-participating brothel manager and card dealer at Sam's House of Pleasure, about three blocks from the hotel. Madame La'fay had been a masterful and highly skilled poker player and card shark since her teen years in Louisiana. She never dressed the part of a bordello madam, but instead was an exquisitely suited card dealer complete with a front holster six-shooter. She insisted on neat, clean and sexy girls that mixed well with the saloon customers. Her rules were strict. None of her girls were allowed to go upstairs with a gentleman without her approval. With gentlemen she did not previously know, she insisted on interviewing them, as to their cleanliness and temperament. Her girls must above all, be treated as ladies.

By the time Captain Frank and the other men had skirted Richmond, keeping to the back-roads, five of the men had broken off and headed toward their homes. Captain Frank and his companion, Will Skinner, about halfway between Richmond and Liberty, were unexpectedly accosted by a small band of eight Union Redlegs. The Redlegs harassed the two men, tied their hands behind their backs and led them to a nearby bean tree. They threw two ropes over a large over-hanging limb, fabricated a slip-knot noose at the end of each rope and placed them over Captain Franks and Will Skinners head. Boisterously laughing and guffawing, they put them on two of their horses and began to pull the ropes taught. Captain Frank, not ready yet to buy the farm this close to home was about to flank kick the horse in a rational attempt to jerk the rope out of the Redlegs hands, when out from the thicket behind them, like a tumultuous hurricane road six men with guns blazing. The murderous Union Redlegs were all dead before they could pull their weapons.

A tall man wearing a black suit rode up and took the rope from Captain Dunbar's neck and untied his hands as another did the same for Will Skinner.

"Frank James!" exclaimed Dunbar. "Man, am I ever so glad to see you, I thought we were goners for sure, I was sayin' my prayers and scared as all getout."

"Yes Franklin, I can imagine." Frank said, knowing it was Franklin Dunbar by his bright blue piercing eyes hidden behind a heavy beard. "Y'all should have scrapped those Confederate uniforms a long time ago. The woods are full of Redlegs and Union militiamen that think the war is still going on. Y'all get off of them Union saddles and ride up behind us. We'll go over to Mama's and get'cha some clothes and hosses. You know my brother Jesse," he motioned to Jesse. "This here is Cole, John, Jim and Bob Younger."

"Hi, Mister Dunbar, It's certainly good to see'ya." Jesse yelled. "Tell Junior hey when ya'see'em," Jesse, walked around among the Union Redleg soldiers shooting each one again in the head.

"This other man here is Will Skinner." Dunbar said.

"Yeah," said Cole. "Will is almost our next door neighbor down in Jackson County."

Dunbar got up behind Frank, and Will behind Cole, and they left toward Kearney and the farm of Dr. Reuben Samuel and Zerelda James-Samuel, Frank and Jesse's mother. There they were each given clothes and a horse. Captain Frank would never know that the James's and Younger's were on the way home from robbing the Richmond Bank when they saved him and Will from hanging.

Chapter 2

Frank and Jesse, as times were, after participating in guerrilla warfare under Quantrill and Anderson, had decided to follow the path of outlawry, owing to the reasoning that it was their dealt hand to do so. From what the Union had done to their way of living, they deduced that they would better themselves by robbing banks and trains that were either owned or belonged by association to the Union. Frank and Jesse knew from experience that former members of the Confederate army, and especially former guerrillas, had to lead wary lives in postwar Missouri.

Jesse James did not become famous until December 1869, when he and Frank, along with their cousin Wood Hite, and other former guerrillas robbed the Daviess County Savings Association in Gallatin, Missouri. The robbery netted little money, but it appears that Jesse shot and killed the cashier, Captain John Sheets, mistakenly believing him to be Samuel P. Cox, the militia officer who had killed "Bloody Bill" Anderson before the war was over. Jesse's self proclaimed attempt at revenge, and the daring escape he and Frank made through the middle of a posse shortly afterward, put his name in the newspapers for the first time.

The 1869 robbery marked the emergence of Jesse James as the most famous of the former guerrillas turned outlaw. It marked the first time he was publicly labeled an "outlaw", as Missouri Republican Governor Thomas T. Crittenden set a reward for his capture. This was the beginning of an alliance between Jesse and John Newman Edwards, a former Confederate cavalryman. Six months after the Gallatin robbery, Edwards published the first of many letters from Jesse James to the public asserting his innocence. Over time the letters gradually became more political in tone, denouncing the Republicans and voicing Jesse's pride in his Confederate loyalties. Together with Edward's admiring editorials, the letters turned Jesse into a symbol of Confederate defiance of Reconstruction.

The James brothers joined with Cole Younger and his brothers, as well as Clell Miller, Wood Hite, and other former guerrillas to form what came to be known as the James-Younger gang with Jesse as the public face of the gang. The gang carried out a string of robberies from Iowa to Texas and Kansas to West Virginia and Arkansas into Louisiana.

Franklin Dunbar, a slender handsome man just under six feet with a strapping muscular physique and bright sharp blue eyes, sat on a cane bottom chair next to the bath-tub with a towel across his lap as Madame La'fay trimmed his black hair to shoulder length, and cut his beard short before starting to shave his face.

Madame La'fay had not gone to work that day, due to the saddening news of her son's probability of being killed. She had finished a late breakfast in the hotel restaurant and was about to enter the elevator in the hotel lobby to go to her apartment when a heavily bearded man in baggy clothes approached the elevator. On a second glance at his blue eyes, she had screamed with wondrous excitement, and grabbed the man tightly. Crying with joy she tried to kiss him through the beard.

"Frank, Frank, Frank darling, it's really you, you've come home." She stepped over to the desk and told the man she needed a tub of hot water in her apartment as soon as possible, "My husband is home from the war," said she, crying joyously.

"Where in the world did you get those baggy clothes?" asked La'fay.

"My uniform was beginning to get battle worn and uncomfortably risky to wear. It was seemingly about to suppress me. Will Skinner and I stopped up at the James farm and Dr. Reuben gave us clothes and hosses to come home on. She's a nice little Roan mare. I left her at the livery. We will return her one day soon, and visit."

"How did you find Mrs. Zerelda and the girls?"

"Everyone was fine, they send their best to you and said come to see them. Frank and Jesse were there too."

"How does Dr. Samuel manage to keep his farm from being burned by the damnable Yankee militia?"

"They've been having their troubles. They were made to leave the state about a year ago, or be burned out and killed. They went over into Nebraska for a few months. Some of their loyal freedmen stayed to keep the farm from running down. Only two of them had left and joined the Union's Negro brigade. They are always on edge not knowing what might happen."

La'fay got the soap dish and began to lather a brush.

"Baby-doll, it's been four long years and I'm in dire need of some of your sweet loving—could not this shaving wait?"

"You know, it's been four years for me too, but we are going to get you cleaned up first. You can wait a little while. You know that's the one thing you can get the furthest behind on and catch up the quickest of anything in the world. So you just be patient."

"But Baby-doll," he said, "hurry, I may have forgotten how."

She chuckled as she began lathering his beard. "Don't you worry, I'll teach you." Madame La'fay thought it best to hold up on telling him about Junior until she welcomed him home and relieved him of his inhibitions. She loved her man greatly and dreaded telling him about their son. She decided to wait until morning.

Adorning himself in one of his old suits complete with double-stitched sailcloth suspenders, and renting a carriage from the livery with a fine pair of Arabian carriage horses, Frank and La'fay were in Fort Osage before noon.

"If your son was one of the dead ones," Major Montgomery said, "he is buried on the backside of the Fort in a community grave. None of that bunch ever carried identification, so I can't tell you the names. I can say that I believe we got them all in that skirmish. Would you care to visit the gravesite?" They declined and left the Fort bearing painful and heartbroken recollections of their beloved son. Frank had thoughts of getting his pistol from under the carriage cushion and killing Major Montgomery. Only his love for La'fay checked his intemperate anger. He knew without a doubt that if he killed him, they would both suffer a violent death.

Back home they looked at some tintypes of Junior as he grew up on their Clay County, Missouri tobacco, ribbon cane syrup, and hemp farm. They lived on the farm until the talk of war became a reality, at which time they sold all of their farming equipment and livestock, except for Frank's saddle horse, and moved into the hotel in Kansas City. Junior at that time was fourteen years old.

While Frank related his sorrow and disgust of the Union's Reconstruction Administration's handling of the Congressional and State offices being seated entirely with Republicans, and many of them Negro, with not even one Democrat being seated anywhere in any southern states, La'fay did her best to console him and take his mind off of it.

In 1861, Lincoln justified the war in terms of legalisms (the Constitution was a contract, and for one party to get out of a contract all the other parties had to agree), and then in terms of the national duty to guarantee a "republican form of government" in every state. That duty was also the principle underlying federal intervention in Reconstruction. In his Gettysburg Address Lincoln redefined the American nation, arguing that it was born not in 1789 but in 1776, "conceived in Liberty, and dedicated to the proposition that all men are created equal." He declared that the sacrifices of battle had rededicated the nation to the propositions of democracy and equality, "that this nation shall have a new birth of freedom—and that government of the people, by the people, for the people, shall not perish from the earth." By emphasizing the centrality of the nation, he rebuffed the claims of state sovereignty. While some say Lincoln moved too far and too fast, they agree that he dedicated the nation to values that marked "a new founding of the nation."

During the Civil War, Lincoln appropriated powers no previous President had wielded: he used his war powers to proclaim a blockade, suspended the writ of habeas corpus, spend money before Congress appropriated it, and he wrote and passed an unconstitutional 13ᵗʰ amendment to the Constitution. Constituted a Federal takeover of all financial institutions, and urgently negotiated with state leaders in Maryland, to not secede from the Union, promising them that he would not interfere with slavery in their state, knowing all the while that he was lying.

On April 12, 1861, the Civil War began and eventually eleven Southern states seceded from the Union. In Maryland, the slaveholder portion of the population favored joining the Confederate States of America. Because the threatened secession of Maryland would leave the Federal capital of Washington D.C., an indefensible enclave within the Confederacy, Lincoln suspended the writ of *habeas corpus* an imposed martial law in Baltimore and portions of the state, ordering the imprisonment of pro-secession Maryland political leaders at Fort McHenry and the stationing of Federal troops in Baltimore. Although Maryland remained in the Union, newspaper editorials and many Marylanders agreed with Supreme Court Justice Roger B. Taney's decision in Ex parte Merryman that Lincoln's actions were unconstitutional.

President Lincoln had been assassinated while Captain Franklin Dunbar was on his way home. John Wilkes Booth, a well-known actor and a Confederate spy from Maryland, unaware of the Amnesty Proclamation of December 8, 1863, had formulated a plan to kidnap Lincoln in exchange for the release of Confederate prisoners. After hearing an April 11 speech in which Lincoln promoted voting rights for blacks, an incensed Booth changed his plans and determinately decided to assassinate the President.

Being strongly opposed to the abolitionist who sought to end slavery in the U.S., Booth had attended the hanging on December 2, 1859, of abolitionist leader John Brown, who was executed for leading a raid on the Federal Army at Harpers Ferry. Booth had been rehearsing at the Richmond Theatre when he abruptly decided to join the Richmond Grays, a volunteer militia of 1500 men traveling to Charlestown for Brown's hanging, to guard against an attempt by abolitionist to rescue Brown from the gallows by force. When Brown was hanged without incident, Booth stood in uniform near the scaffold and afterward expressed great satisfaction with Brown's fate, although he admired the condemned man's bravery in facing death stoically.

On the morning of Good Friday, April 14, 1865, Booth went to Ford's Theatre to get his mail, where he was told by John Ford's bother that President and Mrs. Lincoln accompanied by General and Mrs. Ulysses S. Grant would be attending the play *Our American Cousin* at Ford's Theatre that evening. He immediately set about making plans for the assassination which included making arrangements with livery stable owner James W. Pumphrey for a getaway horse and an escape route. Booth informed his associates Lewis Powell, David Herold and George Atzerodt of his intention to kill Lincoln. He assigned Powell to assassinate Secretary of State William H. Seward and Atzerodt to assassinate

Vice President Andrew Johnson. Herold would assist in their escape into Virginia.

By targeting Lincoln and his two immediate successors to the office, Booth seems to have intended to decapitate the Union government and throw it into a state of panic and confusion. The possibility of assassinating the Union Army's commanding general as well was foiled when Grant declined the theatre invitation at his wife's insistence. She wished to leave for Chicago to visit relatives.

As a famous and popular actor who had frequently performed at Ford's Theatre, and was well known to its owner John T. Ford, Booth had free access to all parts of the theatre, even having his mail sent there. By boring a tiny spy-hole into the door of the presidential box earlier that day, the assassin could check that his intended victim had made it to the play and observe the box's occupants. That evening, at around 10 p.m., as the play progressed, John Wilkes Booth slipped into Lincoln's box and shot him in the back of the head with a .44 caliber Derringer.

He then leaped to the stage and shouted *"Sic simper tyrannis!"* (Latin for *"Thus always to tyrants"*, attributed to Brutus at Caesar's assassination and the Virginia state motto).

In the ensuing pandemonium inside Ford's Theatre, Booth fled by a stage door to the alley, where his getaway horse was held for him by Joseph "Peanuts" Burroughs. The owner of the horse had warned Booth that the horse was high-spirited and would break halter if left unattended. Booth left the horse with Edmund Sprangler, and Sprangler arranged for Burroughs to hold the horse.

A twelve-day manhunt ensued, in which Booth was chased by Federal Agents and cornered in a Virginia tobacco barn where he was shot and killed. His accomplices and conspirators, boarding house owner, Mary Surratt, and four of seven men were eventually tried and hanged.

Lincoln never regained consciousness and was pronounced dead at 10 a.m. April 15, 1865. Lincoln's body was carried by train in a grand funeral procession through several states on its way back to Illinois. Much of the nation mourned him as the savior of the United States while Copperheads and many Confederate Insurrectionist celebrated the death of a man they considered a tyrant.

Shortly after Booth's death, his brother Edwin wrote to his sister Asia, "Think no more of him as your brother, he is dead to us now, as he soon must be to all the world, but imagine the boy you loved to be in that better part of his spirit, in another world." Asia also had in her possession a sealed letter which Booth had given her in January 1865 for safekeeping, only to be opened upon his death. In the letter, Booth had written: "I know how foolish I shall be deemed for undertaking such a step as this, where, on one side, I have many friends and everything to make me happy—to give up all—seems insane; but God is my judge. I love justice more than I do a country that disowns it, more than fame or wealth."

Booth's letter, seized along with other family papers at Asia's house by Federal troops and published by *The New York Times* while the manhunt was underway, explained his reasons for plotting against Lincoln. In it he said, "I have held the South was right. The very nomination of Abraham Lincoln, four years ago, spoke plainly war upon Southern rights and institutions." The institution of "African slavery," he had written, "is one of the greatest blessings that God has ever bestowed upon a favored nation," and Lincoln's policy was one of "total annihilation."

Chapter 3

After raving and ranting about how Reconstruction was killing and enslaving the people of the southland, Franklin looked at La'fay somewhat piteously.

"I'm sorry Babe-doll—I just get beside myself when I see what's happening to our beloved south. There should be a way to get southern politicians back in office, to make laws for the benefit of the south. If that could be done, then we could all prosper again. It could be done with money—money talks, it's the one dividing denominator. Hell, we would need a gold mine to get that kind of money."

With a hint of astonishment in her tone, La'fay blurted "We have a goldmine."

"What?"

"I said we have a gold mine. I won it in a poker game." She got up and took three legal deeds from a table drawer, signed over to her and notarized by the bank president. One was for a gold mine. One was for a hotel with a restaurant, and one for a saloon.

Franklin looked the documents over with a blank face and then stared at La'fay somewhat dumbfounded.

"There was this little man," she said, "that had been losing money nightly for about a week. He was nervous and sweated a lot. One night he had a good hand in draw poker. I could tell it was good, because he was fidgety and I knew he was almost broke. He excitedly took these deeds from his inside coat pocket and asked me if he could put them up for ten thousand dollars. That was about what he had lost and was hoping to get even."

Franklin continued to stare expressionless at La'fay.

"I looked the deeds over and had the bank president to look at them. He agreed that they seemed to be legitimate."

"You stopped the game and took them to the bank?"

"No, silly—he was at the poker table."

"Oh."

"I ask the man if he was sure he wanted to put them up against the one hand. He said yes, if you will cover them for ten thousand. He said that wasn't even a fraction of their worth. I looked at the certainty in his eyes and told him his bet was covered.—How many cards do you want, I asked him.—I'll play these, he said.—If you're pat, then I'll also play mine.

Turn'em over. He turned over a full house, Aces over Queens—I turned over four Tens. Without saying a word he politely signed over the deeds and the bank president witnessed them. The man's name on the deeds was Oscar O'Brian. The man went upstairs to his room without uttering a word. The next day Sam told me the little man shot himself in the wee hours of the morning. I was horrified." She started to weep.

Franklin got up and embraced her. "There, there Baby-doll—it wasn't any fault of yours. You don't know what kind of problems or worries the man might have had, anyway he may be better off now."

Franklin Dunbar met La'fay Beauxdeen on a trip to south Louisiana to buy some pure ribbon cane sprouts. He had a hankering to raise some cane, build a syrup mill, and can syrup. He already had eighty acres of tobacco, fifteen acres of corn, a grist mill and forty acres of hemp. Except for house servants, Franklin at the young age of twenty-five, lived in a big house alone. Meeting La'fay was a God-send. It was head over heels—love at first sight—for both of them. He met her in a Poker Parlor in Lafayette. Franklin was not a poker player, he stopped in to have a beer and cool off. There she was in all her radiant beauty sitting at a poker table about to get shot in the back of her beautiful head by a disgruntled player. Franklin in one quick leap tackled the gunman and took away his pistol. A local lawman handcuffed the would-be killer and took him away. Before the day was over Franklin had ask her to marry him and live in Missouri. The feeling that she owed him her life had nothing to do with her answer. She knew without a doubt that she loved this handsome blue-eyed man with all her heart.

They lived an ecstatic life of love for fifteen years with their loving son, Junior, on their picturesque Missouri farm before moving into Kansas City at the start of the war. After selling all of their farming equipment and livestock, and getting settled in town, Franklin said his goodbyes to his wife and son, went to the livery, saddled his horse, and left to fulfill his patriotic chore. La'fay went to work at Sam's.

On November 6, 1860, Abraham Lincoln had been elected as the sixteenth President of the United States. He was the first Republican president, winning entirely on the strength of his support in the North: he was not even on the ballot in ten states in the South. The electoral vote was decisive: Lincoln had 180 and his opponents added together had only 123.

With the emergence of the Republicans as the nation's first major sectional party by the mid-1850's, the old Two Party System collapsed and a re-alignment created the Three Party System. It became the stage on which sectional tensions were played out. Southern secessionists read the political fallout as a sign that their power in national politics was rapidly weakening. The Democrats suffered a significant reverse in the electoral realignment of the mid-fifties. They lost the dominance they had achieved over the Whig Party and, indeed, were the minority party in most of the northern states. Abraham Lincoln's election in 1860 was a watershed in the balance of power of competing national and parochial interest and affiliations.

It must be noted that during this time, as opposed to today, the newly formed Republican's seemed to be the dominant left-wing liberal party, and the Democrat's' the right-wing conservatives, excepting for the fact that they were slave owners, as were most Independents.

As Lincoln's election became more likely, secessionists made clear their intent to leave the Union, due to Lincoln's position on slavery as outlined in the Kansas – Nebraska Act of 1854, which expressly repealed the limits on slavery's extent as established by the Missouri Compromise (1820). "The Act," said Lincoln." Has a declared indifference, but as I must think, covert real zeal for the spread of slavery, I cannot but hate it. I hate it because of the monstrous injustice of slavery itself. I hate it because it deprives our republican example of its influence in the world—enables the enemies of free institutions, with plausibility, to taunt us as hypocrites—causes the real friends of freedom to doubt our sincerity, and especially because it forces so many really good men amongst ourselves into open war with the very fundamental principles of civil liberty—criticizing the Declaration of Independence, and insisting that there is no right principle of action but self-interest. On December 20, 1860, South Carolina took the lead; by February 1, 1861, Florida, Mississippi, Alabama, Georgia, Louisiana, and Texas had followed. Soon after, they were joined by the upper South, Delaware, Maryland, Virginia, and North Carolina. Followed by Tennessee, Kentucky, Missouri, and Arkansas. Declaring themselves to be a new nation, the Confederate States of American, they selected Jefferson Davis on February 9, 1861, as their provisional President.

President Buchanan and President-elect Lincoln refused to recognize the Confederacy.

Since Missouri was not yet putting together an Army command, Frank Dunbar rode 600 miles to Nashville, Tennessee, sold his horse, and joined the Tennessee Regulars. On April 12, 1861, Union troops at Fort Sumter were fired upon and forced to surrender. After which, The Regulars wasted no time in getting into the thick of the fighting, where they beat the Yankees at Manasseh, Virginia, (the 1st Bull Run). After only two major battles Franklin Dunbar was promoted to Regiment Captain.

They would again, some two years later, defeat the Union at the 2nd battle of Bull Run. During that two year period the Regulars remained in Virginia fighting in over 170 battles with combined casualties in the tens of thousands, before Virginia split and the northern half became West Virginia. They then went to fight in Tennessee for awhile before going to Pennsylvania for a multitude of battles on the way to their final three days at Gettysburg.

The winters were taking a heavy toll on the Confederate army for lack of food, proper provisions, and sickness. Lee's army was taking boots from dead Yankees, and food was only a dream of the past. Lincoln made Grant commander of the Union Army. Grant then waged his bloody Overland Campaign in 1864 with a strategy of a war of attrition, characterized by high Union losses at battles such as the Wilderness and Cold Harbor, but by proportionately higher Confederate losses. Lee's Army shrank with every battle, forcing it back to trenches outside Petersburg.

After an unsuccessful Confederate assault on Fort Steadman, Lee retreated from Petersburg and reluctantly surrendered to Grant on April 9, 1865, at the Appomattox Court House.

Junior Dunbar asked Sam at the House of Pleasure, where his mother was.

"I'll do declare, you're Junior, ain't'cha—Junior Dunbar. How ya' been' boy?"

"I'm good—just wondering about my mother."

"She and Captain Frank left here eight or ten days ago. They thought you were dead. Yeah, the Major over at Fort Osage said you got killed. They took a train west nearly two weeks ago."

"My Dad was with her?"

"Yeah, he came back from the war—lookin' good, he was—not missin' nary a leg or nothin', really lookin' good."

"Did they say where they were going?"

"Naugh, they just got on the train and left, goin' west."

"Okay, Sam—thanks, maybe I can find out somethin' at the station."

The ticket manager remembered them well. He told Junior that they purchased tickets for themselves and three horses to somewhere in Idaho. They had one horse rigged with pack gear, and two with saddles. "I figured," he said, "they were probably going elk hunting. They had plenty of fire power, four Sharps rifles and a lack number of side-arms."

"Where bouts in Idaho?"

"Let me look back in my book." He thumbed back in his book. "Yeah, here it is. It was to Blackfoot, yeah, Blackfoot, Idaho."

Junior thanked him and walked away completely perplexed. During almost four years of riding roughshod with insurrectionist bushwhackers, Junior had learned to accept unexpected circumstances and not dwell or linger over the consequence.

He was a rather fine looking young man with a pleasing personality, taking after his father more-so than his mother. He had black hair which he kept cropped just above his shoulders, and light hazel eyes with a tint of green which became more pronounced when he was angered or upset. Those who knew him well had learned to steer clear when his eyes showed pronounceable green. So as not to appear as a renegade, he had changed his appearance before going to see his mother. He wore a nice black suit with a button-up vest, and a white open-collar shirt, and black shinned boots. His self-consciousness would not permit him to wear the derby the haberdasher tried to sell him. Instead he purchased a regular off-white rancher's hat. Junior at the time of being shot from his horse by the Union militiamen and rolled down the bushy embankment, had crawled off into the woods and hid. He stayed there with a ball in his left shoulder, until early morning the next day. His faithful horse, a big sixteen hand high stout-hearted red mare who he called girl, had left the road and circled around to where he lay. In the red mare's mind she didn't belong to Junior. Junior belonged to her. She loved him as a horse can love a man, and she was always determined to take special care of him. They made their way through the woods and a section of swampland, as Junior walked enfeebled, while holding on to the saddle. The red mare followed a trail leading to a farmhouse, where Junior collapsed near the well in front of the house. The red mare reared her head and neighed loudly a couple of times.

A man came out the front door and observed the situation. He picked up Junior and took him into the house before coming back out and taking the red mare to the barn. He stalled her separate from his own horses, took off her saddle and bridle, and gave her water and oats. While Junior was out cold, the man, Edward Bolton, took the ball out of his shoulder. His wife, Inez, put some healing balm on the wound and dressed it. Edward went back to the stall and removed a ball for the red mares left rump, washed it and put balm on it to hurry the healing. Being as how a horse's skin is much tougher than a man's, the ball went only about an inch into the flesh. Edward was amassed at how easy the red mare was to work on. She stood still and only had an occasional ripple of the skin. When Junior awakened he was feverish and somewhat delirious. Inez put a few drops of liquid opium in some warm broth and forced it down him. Two days later he awakened feeling much better. Inez made him rest for another four days before leaving for

Kansas City. Edward asked Junior if he was one of Archie's men that were involved in the shooting down the road from Fort Osage. He told him that Archie had been killed. Junior acknowledged seeing him get shot from his horse. Edward gave Junior a little tin of horse balm and told him to wash and put the balm on the red mare's rump until it heals. "Yes," said Junior, "I, over the years have taken three other balls of lead from her. She is a brave and obedient hoss." Edward commented on how smart the horse was to call him outside when they arrived. "And don't get upset when you see the Union flag hanging over the veranda. It's the only way to protect our place. Me and Inez both rode under the command of General Quantrill until he was killed."

Chapter 4

After finding a for-lease sign on the door at their apartment in South Kansas City, Junior had gone to a bath house, cleaned himself up, got a shave, bought the new clothes and went to Sam's House of Pleasure.

Junior Dunbar, not knowing if his parents would stay in the north country or come back, decided not to try to find them, but wait and see if they returned. He remembered when life was dispassionate and the house they had in the country before the talk of war. That was his happiest times and he still relished the memory. He now harbored a deep desire to make something of himself, now that his preceding life was ended. Because of his past experience, he was contemplating the possibilities of joining the Texas Rangers. Junior was aware that the Rangers were made up of mostly Union sympathizers, so he made a trip up into Kansas to a Union military cemetery and found him a new name from a tombstone, just in case of any records being checked. He borrowed the name George Washington Barstow Junior, from a private of his own age.

In San Antonio, Texas, headquarters of the Texas Rangers, Junior Barstow applied for a job with the Rangers. He was interviewed by Captain Barry Battle. When asked what his qualifications were. He told Captain Battle in no uncertain terms that he could ride harder and shoot straighter than any of his Rangers.

"Would you be willing to prove that to me?"

"Yes Sir."

"I will have a drill set up out on the practice range. Can you be here after lunch?"

"Yes Sir."

On the practice range there was set up a row of eight bottles on each fence opposite one another with a half-mile road running between the bottles. The bottles were four feet apart at the end of the road. The test was to shoot as many bottles as you could while on a hard run toward and through them.

Junior Barstow was given the rules. He rode the mare to the start position, took a third Navy Colt from his saddle-bag and put it into his waist band. The Captain, and some other officers and Rangers were all there to witness the outcome. A starting shot was fired and with Junior's heal prod and voice command the red mare reared up and pushed off on her hind legs into a breakneck speed. Junior started to put the bridle in his mouth as he had done so many times during shootouts with Union militia and Redlegs. He thought better of it for fear of giving himself away. He wrapped the bridle around his saddle pommel, giving the mare free rein, and drew his pistols from their holsters. He didn't fire his guns until he was within thirty feet of the bottles. The spectators thought he wasn't going to fire. The Rangers had always started firing long before. When Junior did fire, with both weapons, it was almost alike to machine-gun fire. He quickly holstered his right gun and drew the one from his waistband, as he passed through and shot six more bottles in rapid succession. He reined up the mare and walked her over to the spectators.

Sixteen bottles, sixteen shots. They all applauded him. That had never before been accomplished.

"Lieutenant Smith," Captain Battle exclaimed. "Issue this man a uniform and sign him up."

"Yes Sir Captain, those Mexicans better sure look out now".

"Private Mathews," the Captain said, "take his hoss to the stable and rub her down."

"If you get on her Private," Junior said with conviction, "don't let those spurs touch her, she will launch you like a rocket." They all looked at Junior's boots and beheld no spurs."

"How do you control her?" the private asked.

"I talk to her."

Captain Battle asked Junior if he always wore two pistols. "Yes Sir Captain, I pack two pistols because I can shoot equally as well with either hand. So if I face off with two men, I still have an equal advantage."

"Ambidextrous huh."

"I recon so, Sir"

The Texas Rangers at this time had trouble controlling the border against renegade Mexican revolutionist who claimed that half of Texas belonged to them.

Ulysses S. Grant (born Hiram Ulysses Grant; April 27, 1822 – July 23, 1885) was the 18 President of the United States (1869 – 1877) as well as military commander during the Civil War and post-war Reconstruction periods. Under Grant's command, the Union Army defeated the

Confederate military and ended the Confederate States of America. Grant began his lifelong career as a soldier after graduating from the United States Military Academy at West Point in 1843. Fighting in the Mexican-American War, he was a close observer of the techniques of Generals Zachary Taylor and Winfield Scott. He resigned from the Army in 1854, then struggled to make a living in St. Louis and Galena, Illinois.

After the American Civil War began in April 1861, he joined the Union war effort, taking charge of training new regiments and then engaging the Confederacy near Cairo, Illinois. In 1862, he fought a series of major battles and captured a Confederate army, earning a reputation as an aggressive general who seized control of most of Kentucky and Tennessee at the Battle of Shiloh. In July 1863, after a long, complex campaign, he defeated five Confederate armies (capturing one of them) and seized Vicksburg. This famous victory gave the Union control of the Mississippi river, split the Confederacy, and opened the way for more Union victories and conquests. After another victory at the battle of Chattanooga in late 1863, President Abraham Lincoln promoted him to the rank of lieutenant general and gave him charge of all of the Union Armies.

On July 25, 1866, Congress, by requisition of President Lincoln, promoted Grant to the newly created rank of General of the Army of the United States. At West Point he had mistakenly been nominated as "Ulysses S. Grant of Ohio". At West Point he adopted this name with a middle initial only. Among colleagues at the academy, his nickname became "Sam", a connotation of "Uncle Sam", which was later destined to be utilized effectively in his presidential campaign.

The influence of Grant's family brought about the appointment to West Point; he himself did not wish to become a soldier. Grant graduated from West Point in 1843, ranking 21st in a class of 39. A portion of Grant's demerits were due to his refusal, at times, of compulsorily church attendance; then a West Point policy that Grant viewed as anti-republican. Although he boasted of never having studied, Grant was so talented at mathematics that after graduation he would have become an instructor in the subject had the Mexican War not occurred. He established a reputation as a fearless and expert horseman, setting an equestrian high jump record that lasted almost 25 years. Although naturally suited for cavalry, he was assigned to duty as a regimental quartermaster, achieving the rank of lieutenant. He helped to manage supplies and equipment.

Preceding the ongoing skirmishes with Mexican revolutionist, Ulysses S. Grant as commanding General of the Army of the United States had to contend with Maximilian and the French army who had taken over Mexico under the authority of Napoleon III. Grant put military pressure on the French Army to leave Mexico by sending 50,000 troops to the south Texas border led by Phil Sheridan. Grant secretly told Sheridan to do whatever it took to get Maximilian to abdicate and the French Army to leave Mexico. Sheridan sent Benito Juarez, the ousted leader of Mexico, 60,000 U.S rifles to aid in an effort to defeat Maximilian. By 1866, the French Army completely withdrew from Mexico, leaving Maximilian to fend for himself. Maximilian, who had been installed as the Emperor of Mexico in 1864, was executed by the Mexican Army in 1867.

After the war, thousands of Irish veterans joined the Fenian Brotherhood and formed the Irish Republican Army with the intention of invading and holding Canada hostage in exchange for Irish independence. In June 1866, Grant went to Buffalo, New York, to assess the situation. He ordered the Canadian border closed to prevent Fenian soldiers from crossing over at Fort Erie and that more weapons be confiscated. In June 1866, the U.S. Army arrested 700 Fenian troops at Buffalo and the Fenians gave up on their attempt to invade Canada.

During Reconstruction, Grant remained in command of the Army and implemented the Congressional plans to reoccupy the South and hold new elections in 1867 with African American voters. This gave Republicans control of the Southern states. Enormously popular in the North after the Union's victory, Grant was elected to the Presidency in 1868. Re-elected in 1872, he became the first president to serve two full terms since Andrew Jackson did so forty years earlier. As president he led Reconstruction by signing and enforcing civil rights laws and fighting Ku Klux Klan violence. He helped rebuild the Republican Party in the South, an effort that resulted in the election of African Americans to Congress and state governments for the first time. Grant's foreign policy, led by Secretary Hamilton Fish, implemented International Arbitration; settled the Alabama Claims with Great Briton and kept the United States out of war with Spain over the Virginius Incident.

On October 31, 1873, a merchant ship, *Virginius,* carrying war materials and men to aid the Cuban insurrection, was taken captive by a Spanish warship. *Virginius* was flying the United States flag and had an American registry; the U.S. did not at first realize it was secretly owned by Cuban insurgents. 53 of the passengers and crew, eight being U.S. citizens, were trying to illegally get into Cuba to help overthrow the government; They were executed, and many Americans, and even Vice President Henry Wilson made impassioned speeches calling for war with Spain.

Hamilton Fish handled the crisis coolly. He found out there was question over whether *Virginius* had the right to bear the U.S. flag. Spain's President expressed profound regret for the tragedy and was willing to make reparations through arbitration. Fish met with the Spanish Ambassador in Washington and negotiated reparations. Spain surrendered the *Virginius* and paid a cash indemnity to the families of the executed Americans. President Grant's Secretary of State, Hamilton Fish, has ranked high among historians, having settled the Alabama Claims and coolly handling the *Virginius* affair.

Despite these civil rights and foreign policy accomplishments, Grant's presidency was marred by economic disaster and multiple scandals in his administration. His response to the panic of 1873 and the severe depression that followed was heavily criticized. His low standards in Cabinet and Federal appointments and lack of accountability generated corruption and bribery in seven government departments. His reputation was severely damaged by the graft trials of the Whisky Ring, when corrupt government officials and whiskey makers stole millions of dollars in a national tax evasion scam. In addition, his image as a war hero was tarnished by the corruption scandals during his presidency.

Chapter 5

Junior Dunbar alias Junior Barstow by 1870 had been promoted to Lieutenant in the Texas Rangers with the dignity of having the highest honor of supreme merit. The back and forth skirmishes with the revolutionist who had inherited the 60,000 rifles sent to Benito Juarez seemed to have no end.

At the end of each summer Junior had gone to Kansas City by train to see if his parents had returned. Three summers had passed with no sign of them. He had a deep feeling of loneliness for his parents. He had thoughts of looking for them, but could not give up his career at this time. He did however ride up to the old farm between Excelsior Springs and Richmond just to see how it looked. The house and barns had been burned to the ground and the land grown up in weeds. On that farm with his Mom and Dad, and through adolescence, had been the happiest days of his life. He had thoughts of going over to Kearney to see about Mrs. James and Doctor Samuel, but thought better of it. This day had been sad enough already. He remembered many good times at the Sunday brush arbor fried chicken dinners, and singings, with Jesse, Frank and Esau Jones. He remembered how Frank couldn't keep his mind off of the girls, and Jesse was the clown of the bunch, always playing tricks on everybody. Esau was the serious perfectionist. At thirteen, Esau was meticulously practicing different ways of fast draw and precise accuracy with his pistol. Junior at times found himself taking lessons from Esau on pistol wielding. Of the four friends Junior invariably considered himself the best singer.

Junior had picked up a habit of daydreaming about his characteristic traits, and constantly had to rebuke himself about it. Little good it did. He remembered how his Dad would reprimand him about daydreaming when they worked together on the farm. His Dad never showed anger or raised a hand to him. He would reprove him verbally, in a caring way, which hurt Junior much more than a good flogging would have.

Some three years before Junior was promoted to Lieutenant in the Texas Rangers, Captain Frank and Madame La'fay had arrived in Blackfoot, Idaho. As La'fay outfitted their packs with needed equipment for traveling horseback, Captain Frank acquired the needed information to find Timberline. With no difficulties they should be there in eight days. They needed no landmarks, for there was a well worn wagon road they had only to follow. It took them on a never-ending ascension around stands of forest and between peaks that reached to the sky. At Fort Hall Reservation in Blackfoot they were told of the possibility of encountering small numbers of renegade Indians, who may try to take their supplies.

Such an encounter did actually occur about midway of their trip. They had no alternative but to shoot three Blackfoot Indians. He reported the fact to the Sheriff in

Timberline that he shot them, but in all actuality La'fay had shot one of them. Madame La'fay, was good with a gun. She sat her horse like a man and could outride most men. From a distant, with her hair under her hat, one could easily mistake her for another cowboy,

Early morning on the last day of travel, they had a breathtaking view of the actual timberline of gigantic evergreen trees stretched in a straight line across the high peak, with baron rock formations rising majestically into the clouds above. They sat on their horses and admired the view for some time before moving on. Another five hours they were in the mining town of Timberline. They dismounted and walked the horses up the street. The town consisted of one long street of businesses and resident tents and lean-to's on both sides. The muddy street was alive with placer-miners, carpet-baggers and charlatans. They came upon a crowd of at least a hundred men scattered up and down the road eating from tin plates and dishes of chipped enamel. Mike's Place was a ramshackle place of stained canvas and poles. The few tables with benches were overly crowded. "Must be at least a hundred people today," the scrubby-bearded man walking beside them said, "About average for this time of the season. Look at'em," His disgust was evident. "Ain't one in ten knows what he's after or would know a color if he saw it. They'll spend all they brung with'em, and here or there a few will make a little. Most of'em will jump at the chance to move on to any other boom camp, always ready to think the pot of gold is right over yonder hill, but they want to stumble over it, not work for it. Most of'em are looking for something easy, something to find or steal, or what's offered on a platter."

"There must be some good men among them," said Frank.

"Yeah, that there is," said the man.

"And there are some women over there," said La'fay, motioning.

"They aren't your kind," Frank replied, "Stay shy of'em. If you're seen with'em, you're likely to be taken for one of'em."

"Do you think that seems fair?"

"We're not talkin' bout what's fair or unfair. We're talkin' realities. Some of those women would lend you their last dollar or nurse you if you were sick, but there's others what would steal the fillins' from your teeth or give you a knife in the ribs for what's in your pockets."

"On up the road away," the man said, "There is a really nice restaurant and hotel. There ain't none of this kind could even hope to pay their price. It won't be long till they'll be moving on down the mountain. That's the way it is a couple of times ever summer."

By the time they got to the Hotel/Restaurant, miners were constantly carrying water up the road from a mule drawn water-wagon parked near the hotel—water to work their home-made gravel washers. They all had a placer claim along an old exposed ancient riverbed around the mountain from La'fay's and Frank's hard-rock mine.

Frank and La'fay, found the land office and inquired about the deeds. The land office manager, after consulting with the Sheriff, acceded to the validity of the deeds. Sheriff Billy Dunstan took them back to the Hotel/Restaurant that was being run by a man named Parker with his wife and daughter, hired by Oscar O'Brian. The Sheriff introduced the Dunbar's as their new employers. He then took them to the Saloon and did likewise with Jake Winston, who ran the saloon for O'Brian. The saloon had no other name, only a red lettered roughly painted sign, hanging askew across the front stating *saloon*. The bar and tables were packed with riffraff, vermin, and lesser dregs of society which frequents or haunts such a place. La'fay noticed a couple of poker games in progress, and six unfitting dance-hall girls, but did not comment. The Sheriff told Frank that he now owned the only hard-rock mine on the mountain. "It's just up the way a piece from the end of the road and has a complete smelter and foundry. The man's name that is in charge up there is Forrest Abernathy. He'll be down bout supper time. He stays here at the Hotel."

"I assume that O'Brian was not a miner."

"No, Abernathy takes care of the mining. O'Brian hardly ever went up there.—Where is he now?"

"He died in Kansas City, Missouri," said Frank.

"His wife died less than a year ago of consumption," Sheriff Dunstan said. "He's been brooding ever since. I guess it finally killed him."

"Yeah, I guess so—the food sure smells good. Baby-doll, you want to eat supper here?"

"Sure," La'fay said, "we may as well get us a room too, if they have one."

"I'm sure they might find one for the owners of the establishment," chuckled Frank.

"I'll join y'all for supper, with your permission, of course", said the Sheriff.

"Be our guest." Franklin answered good-naturedly.

Sheriff Billy Dunstan was a polite congenial man, muscular and standing six and a half feet tall. Just the sight of him would make most men cower in fear.

"I'll join you," the Sheriff said, "As soon as I speak to the manager, Mister Parker, bout your room."

They were seated at a table when the Sheriff returned. "The room is all taken care of," said the Sheriff.

During supper Forrest Abernathy came in, and with the Sheriff's suggestion, joined them at the dinner table.

"Forrest", the Sheriff said, "This is Mister and Mrs. Franklin Dunbar. No use delaying the inevitable—they are your new boss".

"What happened to Oscar?"

"He died down south in Missouri." said the Sheriff.

"I kind of figured he might." Forrest said. "He constantly mourned over his wife's surmise.—Seems I was always trying to cheer him up, but nothing ever worked. He was always heavyhearted and down in the dumps. How did y'all folks happen by his deeds? I knew he always carried them with him."

"He lost them in a poker game, and Madame La'fay bought them at auction."

"I see." Forrest said. "And y'all come to see what'cha bought, huh?"

"Yeah," said Frank, "somethin' like that."

"Well, you're pretty well lookin' at it. This hotel and restaurant, and the saloon a few doors down. The mine is better'n a half a mile up the road. Y'all come all the way from Missouri, did'ya? This hell-hole ain't fittin' for decent folk to be livin' in. If I knew anything else ceptin' mining I sure wouldn't be livin' here. I was in Deadwood for awhile, back in the Black Hills workin' my own little ole' mine and Oscar came there and talked me into coming here and running his mine. I came out'ta one hell-hole right into another."

"How's the mine puttin' out, Forrest? Is it givin' up any gold?"

"We're beginnin' to get some now. For a while there we was only breakin' even. You know it takes money to run a hard-rock mine. Plus I have five workers I have to pay. One of'em is a night watchman and one is a day watchman. The other three work in the mine with me. We just recently broke into an alluvium deposit and are beginning to do pretty good."

"What is this alluvium deposit?

"It's a deposit of river washed rocks, you know, like you find in a river bed. It's from an ancient river bed, and we broke into it right at the bottom of the alluvium at the old river's bedrock. I've got the men building a sluice-box to wash the material so we can separate the gold from the sand and rock. We will take up enough water to keep using it over and over in the sluice. So, all of a sudden we are placer miners instead of hard-rock miners. The ideal thing to do would be to bring a water-wagon around the old logging road on the back side of town. We could bring it right up to the mine."

"So you think it's going to pay off pretty good?"

"I know it is, we're already pickin' up nuggets big as guinea eggs, even without the sluice. I'll take ya'up tomorrow and show it ta'ya."

Madame La'fay and Sheriff Dunstan were taking it all in as they ate, without interrupting. La'fay would occasionally slip her husband a smile.

The following morning they all met for breakfast and left right after to go to the mine. In Blackfoot, La'fay had bought and packed a heavy union suit for each of them when she picked up needed equipment and some more ammunition for the side-arms. They were surely welcomed on the cold morning walking up to the mine. They were both decked out in tanned rawhide pants and coats. La'fay wore a hat with her hair tucked under it and a strap under her chin. She had pulled her sidearm around to her hip.

Sheriff Dunstan and Franklin talked together all the way to the mine. Franklin found out that he had only been the Sheriff through the past winter. He had drifted up here from central Alabama from a life of cotton farming. He did not join the Confederate army because he knew in his heart that it would be a losing, as he put it "state of affairs". He said "The Union would have an unbeatable Army that we would be fighting with plow-shares. I did however ride with General Quantrill against Union sympathizers in Missouri and Kansas, before drifting up here."

"How did you get the job as Sheriff?"

"Twern't hard. The town council needed a Sheriff and I applied. The last two had gotten killed and I guess they were desperate."

They had left the timberline a half mile behind as they ascended to the mine. The incline fell back to level ground and they went into the front of a long building about fifty feet wide with a steep roof to safeguard it from snow accumulation. The building housed the smelter, stamping machine and working benches for the designer/engraver with tools and a scale. Forrest Abernathy explained what everything was used for and told the man sitting just inside the door with a double-barrel shotgun that Mister and Mrs. Dunbar were the new owners. The big heavily bearded man got up from his chair and politely shook Franklin's hand while nodding his head to La'fay. "Pleased to meet'cha," he said. "My name is Abner—Abner Goodman. I kind'a look after the place and keep the thief's away. I've got coffee over yonder on the coal-oil stove if y'all want some."

On another bench near the melting pot, Forrest showed them a water bucket half full of gold nuggets from butter bean to guinea egg size that had been picked out of the gravel material before being washed. He then went to the long bench, reached into a wooden box and took out a handful of gold coins in fifty dollar denominations. He handed them each a coin to look at.

"I weighed out the gold planchets and struck these myself from a stamp made for me by an engraver friend that I used to work with at a mine in Nevada. He now works full time at a mine near Del Rio, Texas. Before Nevada, being a Louisianan, he had honed his trade as an engraver at the New Orleans Mint. Being a branch mint of the United States Mint it closed in January 61, when Louisiana seceded from the Union. These coins are 99.9 percent pure 24 carat gold." The gold coins had a line of trees across the center of the head side with a baron mountain ascending above them with the word *Timberline* below the trees and the date 1873 bottom center with stars around the circumference, interrupted around the top by the words *The Great Northwest.* On the reverse side was a bald-eagle with its wings spread and the denomination of *Fifty Dollars* in a semi-circle at the bottom with stars encircling the remaining circumference. "By the way," Forrest said. "He is coming back up here sometime soon to engrave me a stamp for a one hundred dollar coin and for thousand dollar and five thousand dollar ingots." "We melted and coined these from ore before we broke through to the old river-bed. I'm using some of these to pay my workers and buy equipment to build the sluice. If you may be in need of some money, Mister Dunbar—you know it belongs to you."

"No Forrest, I'll only take two coins to look at occasionally. You just keep up the good work, you're doing a commendable job." Forrest handed him two coins and he gave one of them to La'fay.

"When your engraver friend gets here, I would like to meet him."

"Yes Sir, his name is Pierre Beauregard, I'll be sure you meet him."

"Thanks Forrest, and remember you don't have to call me Sir or Mister Dunbar. I'm known only as Captain Frank. I'm a friend firstly and boss secondly."

"Yes Sir, Captain Frank," said Forrest, with a big smile.

Forrest Abernathy was a big red-headed man, though not as big as Sheriff Dunstan. He was condemned to live his life with an unattractive rowdy complexion, and always in need of a shave, although his demeanor was always that of a delightfully congenial man.

Chapter 6

As Commanding General of the United States Army from 1864 to 1865, Grant confronted Robert E. Lee in a series of very high casualty battles known as the Overland Campaign that ended in a stalemate siege at Petersburg. During the siege, Grant coordinated a series of devastating campaigns launched by William Tecumseh Sherman, Philip Sheridan, and George Thomas. Finally breaking through Lee's trenches at Petersburg, the Union Army captured Richmond, the Confederate capital in April 1865, and Lee surrendered to Grant at Appomattox. Soon after, the Confederacy collapsed and the Civil War ended, consummating the lives of some 750 thousand Americans. That amounts to three times more casualties than any other war in the history of the United States, including both world wars, Vietnam and Korea, Iraq and Afghanistan. It was Americans against Americans, brothers against brothers, the most senseless and shameless war ever to be brought on by a so-called civilized society. Although comrades of defeated Confederate commander Robert E. Lee denounced Grant in the 1870's as a ruthless butcher who won by brute force, most historians have hailed his military genius.

Grant had a difficult relationship with President Andrew Johnson, who preferred a moderate approach to Reconstruction of the South and was increasingly at swords-point with the Radicals in Congress. Johnson tried to use Grant to defeat the Radical Republicans by making him the Secretary of the War "ad-interim" in place of Edwin M. Stanton. Under the Tenure of Office Act, Johnson could not remove Stanton without the approval of Congress. When Congress reinstated Stanton as Secretary, Grant handed over the keys to the War Department and continued his military command. On January 14, 1868 Johnson launched a media campaign to discredit Grant over giving the War Department to Stanton, stating Grant had been deceptive in the matter. Grant, however, defended himself in a written response to the President, made public knowledge, and increased his national popularity. Stanton's return to office and Grant's curt response to Johnson made him a hero to the Radical Republicans, who gave him the Republican nomination for President. He was chosen as the Republican Presidential candidate at the 1868 Republican National Convention in Chicago; he faced no significant opposition. In his letter of acceptance to the party, Grant concluded with "Let us have peace," which became his campaign slogan.

Anti-Semitism became an issue during the 1868 presidential campaign. Though Jewish opinion was mixed, Grant's determination to "woo" Jewish voters ultimately resulted in his capturing the majority of that vote. In the general election of that year, Grant won against former New York Governor Horatio Seymour with a lead of 300,000 votes out of 5,716,082 votes cast. Grant commanded an Electoral College landslide, receiving 214 votes to Seymour's 80.

When he assumed the presidency, Grant had never before held elected office and, at the age of 46, was the youngest person yet, elected President.

In their hotel room after visiting the mine, Frank and La'fay confabulated their state of affairs.

"One thing's for sure." Frank said. "It will take forever to save enough gold to accomplish my desire of returning the south to southerners."

"I certainly don't want us to have to live here for a long time." La'fay said. "I've never even known that such an un-Godly place existed."

"I sure don't want you to play poker here. By the looks of some of these people, they would kill for a dime."

"Don't worry darling, I saw enough when we went to see the saloon. I won't be going back there. I wish we were home on the farm—maybe someday we can rebuild—what are you doing?"

"I'm getting out of this union-suit, I'm getting hot."

"It is getting warm, isn't it." she too, began to undress.

"Why don't you talk to Parker about running the front desk. That would give you something to do, and you wouldn't have to leave the hotel."

"What makes you think I want something to do?"

They laughed, embraced and fell across the bed.

Frank and La'Fay decided to be useful and help out at the mine. Six weeks passed with La'fay sitting at a table weighing the unstamped coin planchets to make sure they were the proper weight before stamping. She would carefully file the planchets down to the proper weight, making sure she kept the gold dust on a sheet placed on the table for saving the filing dust. Forrest told her the job was referred

49

to as being an adjuster. He said some of the big mints that coin gold have as many as 30 adjusters working full time. She and Frank had taken right to the routine of coining gold. For three weeks everything had gone well. Frank had bought a full water wagon with two mules and brought it up the old logging road behind town. They set it right in front of the mine opening ahead of the smelter building and connected a hose from the bottom end of the tank to the sluice. The hose ran downhill into the mine and when turned on at the wagon tank, the water went into the top of the sluice by gravitational force.

The one bucket of nuggets that they first saw had now multiplied to five buckets and they had not yet cleaned the sluice to see what was caught behind the riffles.

Before dark set in, all the people from the mine had gone into town for supper. As they ate, Forrest's friend Pierre Beauregard, from Del Rio, walked into the restaurant. Forrest jumped up and embraced him.

"Hey everybody," he exclaimed, "this is my very good friend Pierre Beauregard. He has come all the way up here to engrave us some stamp heads."

Frank and La'fay got up to meet him. Forrest introduced them to Pierre as the new owners of the mine and they all sat down. The waitress immediately set him a plate and he began to eat like he was starved.

"Mister Beauregard," Frank asked. "You did not ride all the way up from Del Rio, did you?"

"No Sir, although it would have been an invigorating trip with summer coming on.—No, I rode the Union Pacific up to Des Moines and connected with the Great Northern Flyer to Blackfoot. I brought my two horses with me. By the way, Forrest, I have valuables on my pack horse. Will they be safe in the livery?"

Forrest motioned for one of his men to retrieve the pack gear and told Mister Parker to assign him a room. Parker called Forrest to the side.

"Mister Abernathy, if we let anymore free-gratis rooms, Mister Dunbar won't make any money from his hotel."

"Parker, don't you worry about Captain Frank making money from the hotel. I give you my word, it's alright. Give my man with his gear a room number to take it to."

"Yes Sir."

A bit later Parker gave Forrest the key to room 10 and told him Mister Beauregard's gear was in his room.

Pierre Beauregard was a small wiry and agile man, good natured and quick to laugh. One could tell by his perceptiveness that he was an intelligent man. Frank noticed that he had somewhat of a nervous fixation about his little round wire-rimmed eye-glasses. He would fidget with them as he listened intently to whomever was speaking.

"Do you miss Louisiana?" asked Sheriff Dunstan.

Pierre Beauregard looked at him intently before answering. "It would be hard to express my desire of being home in Louisiana. But sometime unjustifiable circumstances command we be elsewhere. For now I have to be where my calling sends me. But yes, I had much rather be in my beloved Louisiana."

"Yeah, like me," the Sheriff said. "I'd rather be in Alabama."

"We have another Louisianan in our midst, Pierre," Forrest said. "Right over there," he motioned. "Madame La'fay Beauxdeen de Dunbar."

La'fay stood, smiled, and extended her hand, Pierre got up, walked around the table, bowed, took her hand in his and gently kissed it.

"Madame Beauxdeen de Dunbar," Pierre said. "We must exchange stories sometime."

"Yes, I shall be delighted," said La'fay in a sweet southern drawl.

"There has never been such elegance portrayed in the hell-hole of Timberline. This is truly a first." Sheriff Dunstan dramatized.

Shortly after sun-up, all of the same people were gathering at the restaurant for breakfast, except for Forrest Abernathy. The crew from the mine had finished eating and Mrs. Baker gave one of the men a food bucket and a container of gravy to take back for Abner Goodman. The mine workers stayed at the mine at night where they had bedrolls and bunks, but came to the hotel for breakfast.

Forrest came down from his room and joined the others.

"Good mornin' my friends—what's for breakfast this lovely mornin'?"

"Well, Forrest," Sheriff Dunstan said. "You could not find a better breakfast this side of Alabama. We have hot biscuits, fried eggs, salt cured fatback, fried crisp, and soppin' flour gravy. Ya'better dig in, fore it's all gone."

"Pierre," Forrest asked. "Tell us the news from the outside world. We never get any news up here. Has the country fallen apart yet?"

"You pretty well hit the nail on the head, Forrest. The country has gotten deeper into a depression than it's ever known. President Grant's reputation has been severely damaged by corruption and bribery scandals in several government departments."

"What about Reconstruction," asked Captain Frank. "How is it progressing? Is the Union militia still in control?"

"Hasn't anything changed Captain, Grant is personally leading the Reconstruction by the signing and enforcement of civil rights laws, while at the same time fighting Ku Klux Klan violence. He is building the Republican Party in the South with the placement of Republicans and African Americans to all state government positions from governor on down. Low standards in his Cabinet, and favoritism in Federal appointments,—and lack of accountability has generated corruption and bribery in most government departments. Our problems only worsen with Republicans running the South."

"Do you think we'll ever be able to do anything about it?" ask Captain Frank with a quivering anger in his voice. La'fay laid her hand on his trembling arm in a consoling manner.

"It doesn't look good Captain," Pierre replied. "But it's alike to any problem,—it won't change unless somebody takes the initiative to do something about it."

"Do y'all won't me to go help out at the mine today?" asked Sheriff Dunstan.

"If it's alright with all concerned, and seeing as how there are only the five of us left in the restaurant. I would allow that we should stay awhile and let me tell you another story. I'm sure you will find it of some importance with enormous possibilities, considering all here are of southern freedom mercenary background, or might I say—freedom fighters." said Pierre with a true seriousness to his voice.

All listened intently to Pierre, and waited enthusiastically for him to continue. Pierre poured him some more coffee, took a sip, and looked fixedly at each individual person before continuing. "As you all know, I have been employed at a large gold mining and minting facility on the Mexican border near Del Rio, Texas. In my capacity there I was privy to about everything that went on. As a result of this privilege, I learned, and know of all the details of an enormous gold shipment, of four billion dollars, to leave there by rail during the second half of September.—Now, what is of importance is the fact that the gold, minted in U.S. coins of all denominations, belongs to the United States—bought by President Grant, and is destined for Washington D.C. to the U.S. Mint there. Further knowledge is that the President, bought the gold from the mine with money borrowed from a conglomerate of U.S. banks, to be used in part to cover promissory notes and greenbacks that are backed by gold.—Now, I can see the wheels turning in Captain Frank's mind.—I will add a few thoughts. The railroads are closed going north throughout the country. Oh, they all are still there. They are just closed down.— Now, due to gate times at the mine and east bound train schedules, the boxcar will have to be sidetracked over night awaiting the midmorning train the following day. Starting mid-month one could watch for the side-tracking of the boxcar. The boxcar will be accompanied by a Pullman car with a troop of Union soldiers to guard the gold. Now there would be a lot of details to be worked out—but just think of the possibilities of stealing that boxcar of gold and bringing it north on a closed track and re-minting the gold as private money. It is my opinion that it could be done with a handful of well trained guerrilla fighters. Billy could take a bunch of fifty dollar gold pieces, catch the flyer across to Missouri and put out a clarion call for some of his old friends. As you have probably imagined by now, I have been reflecting on the possibilities of this scheme all the way from Del Rio."

Sheriff Billy Dunstan immediately spoke up "I'm ready as soon as we get the details all worked out."

"That's going to all be up to Captain Frank," Pierre said. "It's his show. He's the boss. This is May—we only have until September to detail the job and fill in the incidentals," said Pierre, as he looked at Captain Frank for his reaction.

"I'll get right to work on it," Frank said. "You know, above all else, there must be absolute secrecy at all levels. This can only be accomplished if done by a close-knit league of insurrectionist devoted to the sole purpose of instituting the re-birth of our beloved homeland.

Chapter 7

Being the second President from Ohio, Grant was elected as the 18th President of the United States in 1868, and was re-elected to the office in 1872. He served as President from March 4, 1869, to March 4, 1877. He was the first U.S. President to be elected after the nation had outlawed slavery and given citizenship to former African American slaves by U.S. constitutional amendments. Although Grant desired economic expansion and a productive citizenry, his Presidency from the start had to contend with Ku Klux Klan violence, Native American conflicts between settlers in the West, and an unsuccessful attempt to annex Santa Domingo.

Reconstruction dominated most of Grant's presidency, with sectional riots over the status of what the new freedman would have in post-Civil War society. Booming post-war industrial markets and the expansion of the American West fueled wild speculation and corruption throughout the United States, only to come to an abrupt crash with the Panic of 1873. National wounds brought on by the massive socio-economic upheaval of the Civil War continued. Grant's innovative "Peace" policy advocated Native

American citizenship and denounced wars of extermination as "immoral and wicked."

Although there were initial scandals in his first term, Grant remained popular in the country everywhere but in the southland. He was re-elected a second term in 1872. His notable accomplishments as President include the enforcement of Civil Rights for African Americans in the Reconstruction states, the Treaty of Washington in 1871, and the resumption of Specie Act in 1875. Grant's personal reputation as President suffered from the continued scandals caused by many corrupt appointees and personal associates and for the ruined economy caused by the Panic of 1873. Grant's determination was to create and maintain a Republican Union with only Republicans in every Congressional and State level offices. However, a faction of the Republican party, the Liberal Republicans, bolted in 1872; publicly denounced the political patronage system known as Grantism and demanded amnesty to Confederate soldiers. As more scandals were exposed during Grant's second term in office, his personal reputation was severely damaged.

After weeks of working on details for the Leagues first major operation, Billy Dunstan was in Jackson County Missouri visiting with Cole Younger and his brothers.

"Yeah, Billy," Cole said. "We will certainly help out with something as important as this. We've been riding with Jesse and Frank on some robberies, but we can certainly forego that. I'll gather up some of the old boys and meet you back here in two weeks. I'm sure they will be ready. Most of them are still killing Redlegs and Militiamen quite regularly. There is talk of the Yankees sending in the regular army on us."

"Okay Cole, in two weeks. Good to see you're doing well."

"How many men you think it might take," asked Cole.

"Let's go with bout thirty. We'll have to steal a locomotive."

"Okay."

Dunstan handed him a leather pouch with twenty Timberline fifty dollar gold pieces in it.

Cole weighed the pouch in his hand.

"We don't really need this Billy, we're pretty well healed."

"Some of the men you get may need help," said Billy as he mounted his horse and rode away.

About the same time back at the mine in Timberline, Captain Frank, Pierre, Forrest and La'fay were making plans.

"I think our best bet would be to make a bunch of the fifty dollar pieces for expenses, and only engrave and make stamp heads for ten thousand dollar ingot bars to do business with. If we only had more presses we could move much faster."

"Listen," Forrest said. "I know of the ideal place to hide the train, and I believe we could salvage some presses there. That's where I got my fifty gallon melting pot from."

"We're listening Forrest," said Pierre.

"Oh yeah, It's an old abandoned open-pit mine, down close to the ice caves. It's been abandoned for years. They went off and left everything intact. It's called the Lucky Basin Mine, near Hailey. It's only bout four or five days away. We go through the forest southwest till we hit the valley and turn south bout half a day to Hailey.

"Let's leave in the morning," Pierre said. "We'll take a pack mule with us in case we find some presses. La'fay, if you wish, you can weigh some more fifty dollar planchets while we're gone."

"Nothing doing," she said. "I'm going with you."

"A true Louisianan," Pierre laughed. "Got'ta get in the act."

"If we don't watch her," laughed Frank. "She'll be trying to help steal the train."

"That has crossed my mind," she mused, "we all better get a good night's sleep before we head out."

"Yes," replied Frank. "I could use some rest, let's head to the hotel, Baby-doll."

In their room, La'fay poured a basin of water and laid out wash cloths and towels before starting to remove her boots.

"Al'right Baby, let's have it," Frank said. "Just when did you talk to Pierre?"

"What are you talking about?"

"You know what I'm talking bout. Pierre knew right off about my passion for returning the south to the people, and that I was looking for a way to accomplish such an undertaking—now, tell me when did you talk to him."

"Damn, I just can't put anything over on you. I was only trying to be of some help. We sat in the upstairs lounge last night while y'all were still talking in the restaurant—it seems he's all for helping the situation—don't you think?"

Frank starred undoubtedly at La'fay for a moment before cracking a smile. "That boxcar of gold is really somethin' ain't it. Just exactly what we need—how did you read Pierre, do'ya think he's on the up and up?"

"Oh yeah, he wants the south re-born as much as you do."

La'fay was gladdened to see a joyous expression return to her man's face. His prior, dubious and somewhat insecure disposition had worried her immensely. His old positive, self-assured demeanor, much to her liking, had now surfaced again.

After lining out what he wanted the hired help to do at the mine. Forrest took one of the water wagon mules from the corral on the far side of the smelter building and rigged him with side bags for use as a pack mule. La'fay had asked Mrs. Parker to pack a bag of pan-bread and fried salt-back to take on the trip. Frank, La'fay, Pierre and Forrest packed their bedrolls and tied them behind their saddles. They all carried rifles and side-arms. Without saying anything they mounted. Forrest gave the mule a tug and they began the trip bearing to the west through the timber, and holding to a steep downward ravine around a mountain crevasse, dropping considerably in altitude. For at least a terrifying five hours they had to descend a rocky ledge in single file leading the horses and the mule. After another two less erratic hours the route favorable mellowed to a lowland rocky valley where traveling became much easier. They traveled each day until just before dark and made camp. On the third day the land had leveled to a flat plain where they picked up an old unused railway that turned out of the west and bore due south. They followed the railway until dark and again made camp. They talked about the fact that they had not encountered any renegade Indians. Although

Frank's mind was grinding full time, they didn't talk about their plans. They waited to see what they might find at their destination. They all ate some pan-bread but could not take more fried salt-back. It made them drink too much water from their water canvases which caused them to have to stop too much.

About noon on the fourth day there it was. A big tall weathered building at least two-hundred feet long with a spur track leading through the closed door. Down the way a bit they could see the track leading off the main track and the switching implement beside the track. They crossed the track and rode up to the building crossing over numerous other tracks with switching implements. After swinging the big double door open they rode their horses along beside the rail-track into the building. Some birds fluttered and flew out under the open air roof, squawking about the intrusion.

Forrest explained to the others that the track went all the way to the far end of the building and was used for ore cars to bring ore in from the nearby open-pit mine. He said that when the ore was processed, removing the gold, the same train of cars would be loaded with the tailings and taken to a dumping area. Then another train of ore cars would move in. "That's why," he said, "There are so many tracks running around the area outside."

They tied their horses and began to look around. Further into the building, Pierre was ecstatic to find four more round fifty gallon melting pots like the one in the Timberline mine. He noticed that one had been taken out. The pots are individually situated off the ground supported by A-frame mounts with s steel bar running through a vertical stanchion across the top so the pot can be tipped by a large handle. There is a drain pipe coming out of the side of the pot near the bottom with an open and close handle to control the issuing of minute amounts of hot gold for the measuring of planchets. They each are situated over an open pit burner fueled by coal or pine wood.

"Forrest," Pierre asked. "How in God's name did you get that melting pot up to Timberline?"

"I sure didn't take it up the way we came. I had one of my men to help me—I couldn't even lift it by myself, ya'know—anyway we come and got it with a wagon and team of mules. We took it straight east, just north of the craters and intercepted the wagon road bout two days north of Blackfoot."

Pierre stared at Forrest for a long moment without commenting. He then found the stamping table where he hit the jackpot. Four double spring presses, complete with attachment heads and various blank stamps ready for the designer and engraver which he was both. There was a stamping base and three ingot heads which seemed to be the proper size for a 23 pound 6 ounce ingot bar. Considering that gold is measured in Troy weight, and at the price of gold, the stamping base would signify a ten thousand dollar bar, after shaving it a bit less than a half penny-weight at which point it would be the proper weight of 23 pounds and 6 ounces Troy.

In the meanwhile La'fay was gathering fifty dollar size planchet collars and a few ten thousand dollar bar collars. She was filling a canvas bag with these and other useful items like files, brushes and coin holders. Pierre took the base bolts from the presses and put them into another bag. He also retrieved six planchet scales and a bunch of tools.

Once they had scavenged about everything they could, they looked at one another with enthusiastic admiration. There was no need for words.

Forrest was busy looking over the possibility of getting another melting pot. Yes, he thought, *"I will return and get another."* They loaded all of their booty into the pack mule's side-bags and headed home. Once they hit the incline, it was rough going up the side of the ravine, holding to the mountain crevasse along a ridge that seemed to wind straight up. On the morning of the fourth day, tired and living on stale pan-bread, they made it home and went straight to the mine to unload.

At supper time that evening, after cleaning up, they all met and discussed the future. Frank took control and laid out his plan.

He said, "La'fay and I will follow the track south to see if there might be any problems, and if so, how to rectify them. We will keep a log for Billy's people, with any problems they might encounter with switching implements. I am hoping they can by-pass the towns on the main track. That will be for us to see and let the lead man know. I have an idea, and hope, that man will be Cole Younger. It will be a long trip for us. We will return by train from San Antonio, up and over by The Flyer. We may stop off in Kansas City to find out if Billy has made arrangements with Cole, and if the time is going to coincide with the September date. Right now we have a lot of ifs—we just have to work our way through them and hope it all turns out good. I counseled Billy on the importance of letting the men know the purpose of our scheme is for instituting the re-birth of the South to the advantage of helping all southerners in bringing back our old life style that the Union has stripped from us. Billy understands that perfectly and will let the men he gets know that any collusion of differences once we get the gold will not be tolerated, so all should watch each other."

"Captain," Pierre said. "I would if I may, suggest that we stamp a considerable amount of fifty dollar pieces for expenses and then put our efforts into making only the ten thousand dollar ingots,—or bars, in all actuality are what they are. The reasoning behind my suggestion is that there may come the time that you have to deal directly with Grant himself to accomplish your desire. I hate to use the word *blackmail*, so if there be a more plausible word such as maybe *entice*, it wouldn't sound as intimidating—you may have to *entice* Grant to see the reasoning in your favor to help overcome the depression, by the south starting to produce saleable commodities again—and you being a rich man could help with this endeavor. You could offer the government, him, enough gold in installments, to overcome his loss and put him back in good standing. Now, ingots, or bars would be easier and more advantageous for us to make than coins, and they would have to re-mint anyway, to coin the different denominations in U.S. coins that they would need."

"It all sounds very plausible Pierre. That's exactly how we shall handle it."

"Now, there is one other thing," Pierre said. "We will have to use all of our mined gold in the mix with the stolen gold. The reason being that all gold is not the same. The first thing Grant will do on getting a bar of your gold is have his mineralogist examine and test it. Gold along the Mexico border and up through California is a pure buttercup yellow. Gold throughout the Great Northwest, which includes Timberline, has a red tint to it. On over in the Black Hills the red gets more prevalent. So we must hope we can get enough red into the mix of Grant's gold to fool them. I personally think it will work. You know he will be suspicious, being as how he will still be looking for his stolen gold."

"Okay Pierre," Frank said. "I'm glad we have people with us that are more knowledgeable than me. Be sure you keep enough fifty dollar pieces for us to work with. La'fay and I will leave in the morning after breakfast. We should be back sometime in August.—Come late September, our men will have the train on the way to the old mine, Billy will be coming on the Flyer with ten men and horses. We must make arrangements in Blackfoot for forty pack mules, or horses—and someone must meet them to show them the way to the old mine. Also someone will have to intercept the train to show them where to go—at this point it seems we don't have enough people."

Chapter 8

So as to start their journey from the gold train's final destination, Frank and La'fay warily followed the same perilous trail down and around the mountain to the old Lucky Basin Mine. They then began to follow the track south, watching meticulously for any tracking problems. They had hoped to stop in a town, if at all possible, for the nights. About six hours south of Hailey, after spending the night at the Hailey hotel, they passed under the elevated railway of the Great Northern Flyer. Frank calculated it to be approximately 400 miles due west of Blackfoot. A full week southeast near Tremonton, Utah, after sleeping on the ground every night, which certainly was not the resolve of their expectations, Frank and La'fay found the switching implement set to allow the train to take the spur through town. They switched it back to stay on the through track, by-passing the town, and busted the mechanism so it could not be changed. They found the Tremonton Hotel and restaurant to be a welcome place to stay for a couple of days. In another week and a half they had made it to Provo, and had set four more switching implements to by-pass the towns.

In three months of living on jerky, bunking on the ground, and bathing in the streams they had made their way south carefully checking the track through Farmington, Santa Rosa, Roswell and Pecos, winding up at Uvalde, Texas. They evaluated the situation and decided it best to have their train take this first closed track at Uvalde and camouflage it to appear that they had not taken it. La'fay wrote instructions in her log as to the decision of Captain Frank, with an order that whoever reads the log shall burn it.

After a nights rest and a very appreciated hot bath at the Uvalde hotel, they rode into San Antonia, enjoyed a good breakfast and caught the Southern Pacific to Kansas City, Missouri arriving around the noon hour. Once in Kansas City Frank went to the horse car and retrieved their mounts as the railroad wranglers brought them down the ramp. Instead of tightening their chinches, they walked the horses to the livery stable.

"I'd like to put up our mounts for a few days and rent a two up carriage with well trained carriage hosses."

"Yes Sir, Captain. We have the best there is."

Frank was momentarily taken aback. "You know me, do'ya?"

"Yes Sir, I've been here a long time. I know Madame Beauxdeen too, only'est I ain't never seen her in a riding get'up like that."

"Hi Ernest," La'fay said. "It's pleasin' to see you. Has everything been good for you?"

"Yes Mam, just fine."

"Earnest," Frank asked. "I'm lookin' for a man called Billy. Have you heard of such a man. He's big and tall."

"Yes Sir Captain, he's left his hoss here a couple of times." Ernest looked around as if to be secretively and talked low." He was in here a couple of weeks ago with Mister Cole Younger and two more men that I didn't know. I expect he'll be coming back. He stashed his bedroll over yonder in that corner," he motioned to the corner, "I don't expect he'd go off and leave it."

"Ernest," Frank said, "If he returns in the next three days, tell him we will be at the Grand Hotel."

"Yes Sir. Do'ya still won't the carriage?"

"Yes, we will get it in the morning after breakfast."

"Yes Sir."

After checking in to the Hotel and having baths, they went respectively to the haberdasher and ladies boutique, after which they ordered supper in their room and undressed so as to not spoil their new clothing.

"By the way Baby-doll," Frank said, between bites of food, "happy birthday." La'fay only looked expressionless at him, and continued to eat.

"You did know that today is your birthday, didn't you?" said he.

"Yes, I know it, but I'm not admitting to it. You know I told you last year that I was not having anymore birthdays, so I'm still 39 and holding. So now don't say anything else about it."

"Okay Baby-doll, I couldn't think of what to get you, so I'll just forget it." Her feelings were expressed with a scowl.

Attired in their new clothes, and admiring each other, as La'fay straightened the back of Frank's collar, he said, "Looking like dignified high-class folks, we are less likely to be stopped and questioned by damn Yankee militiamen."

"So that was your reasoning for sprucing up. I thought you just wanted us to look good for each other," she feigned pouting. Frank turned and put his arms around her, in a consoling manner.

"There, there, Baby-doll. I did won't us to look good for each other, but I thought it might also help us otherwise."

La'fay suppressed her laughter.

Frank and La'fay, in the two-up carriage took the south road from Kansas City and headed toward Blue Springs.

"You haven't told me where we're going," said La'fay.

"I'm going to see if we can find the Younger place. I know bout where it is, but I ain't never been there."

"Being as how we are going this way, I would like to stop by Blue Springs and see Maria."

"Maria?"

"Yes, Senora Maria Juana Jones—she is a dear friend of mine. I use to visit with her some while you were gone. It could be that Esau might know exactly where the Younger place is. He used to ride with the Younger's under Quantrill and Anderson."

"Esau Jones!" Frank clamored. "The last I heard of Esau Jones was in some dime novels the soldiers were passing around in the camps. He lives at Blue Springs?"

"Yeah, he has a horse farm there."

"You show me where it is. We most certainly will stop."

La'fay showed him the way on the south road down by Blue Springs Lake and up the hill to the gate leading into the Jones Horse Farm. He was extremely flabbergasted at the big anti-bellum style house. La'fay told him to drive around back and stop. Esau's man, Jim Conners came from the barn and took hold of the lead horse.

"Madame La'fay and Captain Frank, y'all folks go on in. I'll take care of the team."

"How did he know who I was?" whispered Frank.

"Maybe he assumed it," answered La'fay.

The back door flew open and Maria ran out exhilarating a squeal of excitement and delight. She hugged La'fay as they danced around the yard jubilantly. Maria was of Mexican descent, very beautiful, somewhat small and shapely with long lustrous black hair and gleaming dark eyes. In her mid-thirties she appeared to be in her early twenties.

"And this is the soldier man I have heard so much about." Maria hugged Frank like they were old friends.

"Come in the house. You all must be thirsty—Esau will be in shortly, he's out in the back pasture."

No sooner than she had said it, Esau rode up, accompanied by his ten year old son. Esau jumped from his horse and hugged La'fay before turning to Frank. He put his hands on Frank's shoulders and gazed seriously into his eyes. They then embraced like two kids and jumped around the yard, whooping and yelling like two drunken Indians. La'fay looked up at the boy and said. "Christian, get down here and hug your aunt La'fay." The boy jumped from his horse and bear hugged her. La'fay introduced the boy to Frank. "Where is your sister, Christine?" she asked.

Maria broke in and said she was at a private cultural school for young ladies, in Independence. "They'll have her home by supper time."

"She is Christian's twin sister." La'fay said to Frank.

"It's been a long time my friend," Esau said. "A lot of water has run under the bridge."

"Yes, it has. I often wondered about you." Frank said. "I lost all track when your books stopped coming out. What happened?"

He pulled Maria to him and hugged her affectionately. "This is what happened. The Lord took pity on me."

They all went in the back of the house laughing."

Esau, directed his speech to Maria and said, "Frank and I used to always go around the countryside with the James's and other friends to the brush arbor church services and singings. Those were the good ol' days. Junior, Frank and Jesse James, and me, used to pretty well take over the singings. We didn't have any cares in the world. There weren't no problems in them days."

"Speaking of problems Esau," Frank asked. "How's things round here with the Union Militia and the Redlegs."

They all sat down around a big dining table.

"Not good at all, Frank." Esau said. Things have gotten worse with the Militia trying to uphold the stupid so-called Congressional Reconstruction. There's recently been a new wave of paramilitary organizations to rise up all across the South. The Red Shirts and the White League that's conducted insurgencies in Mississippi, North Carolina, and Louisiana, operate openly and are more organized than the Ku Klux Klan were. Their aim is to turn Republicans out of office, suppress the black vote, and disrupt elections."

"You know their tactics will never work," said Franklin, "Grant will never be bullied into changing his plans. With him, as the military man that he is, there will have to be a paragon of perfection in the use of strategy." One of the house help came in with a pot of coffee and some cups on a tray. She sat them on the table and said she would be right back with the milk and sugar. Frank poured him a cup as Esau related to his comment.

"You're absolutely right Frank," replied Esau, "In response to the violent outbreaks against African Americans, Grant just recently signed a congressional Civil Rights Act. The legislation mandated equal treatment in public accommodations and jury selection. But nothing was done to allow for Southerners, regardless of political affiliation, to run for office of any kind. The complete make-up of our southland is Republicans and African Americans in virtually every office."

"You've been pretty well keeping up with things, huh?"

"That's about all I have to do now, Frank. The depression is getting so bad hardly anyone can buy a good hoss. The Union Army has been trying to buy my hosses, but there is no way I will sell any of my stock for Army hosses. I did however, in keeping with good terms, tell them that I would be helpful in getting them some wild mustangs from Wyoming, but they would have to do the work, including breaking them. I do sell a good mount occasionally. I sold a nice Red Roan to Frank James recently. Frank always took pride in his riding hoss. I also have sold a few trained carriage teams to people from the North that has heard of the farm. We trained that team you came in with. I saw Jim taking care of them. Sometime I think because I know where to get hosses is the only reason my farm stays intact. I do however, with much remorse, pretend to be a Union sympathizer as the previous owner did. If I didn't I would be burned out. I'm to go to Wyoming before winter sets in with a troop of Union cowboys, ha, to round up some hosses to break and bring back for the Army."

"What I'm doing," Frank said, "is lookin' for Cole Younger, or my man, Billy Dunstan. Have you seen or heard of either of them recently?"

"Yeah Frank," Esau said. "I've seen'em both. They had a meeting here bout a month ago with a whole slew of ex-bushwhackers. I attended the meeting. Billy went through the complete plan and explained to them the purpose of the League as you had set it up. That big man is certainly worth his salt. I know he rode with Quantrill, but I had never met him, as I only started with Bill Anderson, and quit when he was killed. Frank, I was very enthralled with Billy's description of your plan for the rebirth of the south and I want you to know that I'm behind you all the way. Possibly I can be of help in the future with setting up appointments with Union dignitaries as go betweens with Grant, and allowing you and La'fay comfortable surroundings."

Trying not to sound repetitious or unappreciative, Frank said, "I really need to see Cole Younger if you know where to find him."

"The Younger place is bout fifteen miles southeast of us. I'll send Jim to tell him to come and see'ya."

Esau walked out the back door and called for Jim. He told him to go to Cole Younger's and tell him to come see Captain Frank. Jim went and saddled a horse and left. Maria and La'fay had long sense retired to the upstairs. Esau rang a little bell and the same house servant appeared. He told her to bring more coffee and to tell Birdie, that there will be two guests for dinner. He thought of Cole and told her to make that three.

Birdie was putting the food on the table when Jim got back with Cole Younger. Maria and La'fay had returned to the dining room and taken a seat at the table as Christine came in. On seeing La'fay, she ran and hugged her.

"Go upstairs," Maria said to Christine, "and tell your brother to come to supper." After they all exchanged salutations and set down to eat, Frank couldn't wait, He had to know what had been accomplished. Cole being an astute man noticed the apprehensiveness in Frank's face.

"Captain Frank," he spoke calm and quietly. "You may put your soul at rest. All is well. I will be in New Braunfels by the fifteenth of September with thirty well conditioned men who have been masterfully instructed by your Lieutenant Billy Dunstan. I must add that you couldn't have chosen a more perspicacious man than my old friend Billy. Everything should go as planned. The one thing that may cause a hindrance is borrowing a locomotive. We will have to get it in time to build up a head of steam before moving it. But don't you let it bother you. We will work it out. We will be taking our hosses with us. It will be a bit crowded to have them all in one hoss car but we'll just have to tie'em up short.

La'fay reached into her pocket and handed Cole her log of four pages that she had made for the trains journey. Cole spent a good ten minutes looking it over. He then looked at her with admiration.

"Thank you Madame La'fay. I was wondering how I would know when we reached our destination."

The talking stopped as they all put their minds to some needed nourishment. In a few minutes Cole continued.

"Captain Frank," he spoke soft and hesitantly between bites of food. "Billy is at this time picking the ten men to take with him to the rendezvous. His big drawback will be getting forty pack mules, or hosses, to transfer the goods to the mine. He's hoping he can find them in or around Blackfoot. The one last resort would be to steal some hosses from the Army Fort at Blackfoot. But I wouldn't worry, Billy will figure it out. He's good."

Cole Younger thought the world of Billy Dunstan, and for good reason. Billy had saved his skin more than once. He knew Billy to be one of the best guerrilla fighters that ever sat a horse. One story Cole used to like to tell was when he rode abreast of Billy in a skirmish on the road to Rocheport. It was on the morning of September 23, 1864 when about 50 guerrillas were camped near the Howard-Boone line. Another band made rendezvous with them, and soon afterward a courier rode into camp and reported that a group of about ninety Federal militiamen were nearby on the road to Rocheport.

The guerrilla's mounted, reached the main road, and formed ranks of horsemen eight abreast across the route of the Federal company, with Cole and Billy in the center of the front line. Nowhere was the rebel yell given more piercingly than in the wilds of the border country, and when its shriek came from the throats of these guerrilla's, the Union soldiers spines froze and they broke ranks in disorder. Their supply train was captured. Thirty of the militiamen were killed. Darkness saved the rest. Cole always told the story with the indubitable fact that when the shooting started Billy shot so straight and fast that he more than likely saved every man on the front line. The two guerrilla bands were joined the next day by the command of Captain "Bloody Bill" Anderson. It was the intention of the by now sizeable group to join with the force of Confederate General Price, who was marching toward Jefferson City.

When Jayhawkers wantonly sacked the town of Osceola, Missouri, Quantrill's bushwhackers retaliated by laying waste the town of Lawrence, Kansas. It was a day of carnage; More than a hundred men of the town were slain. An ostensible purpose of the Lawrence raid was to find and capture Jim Lane, who had by that time been promoted to General.

Cole Younger, later one of Jesse James's partners in outlawry, was oddly enough, something of a man of mercy that day in Lawrence. He was credited with successfully pleading for the lives of several citizens who were taken prisoner. This act of charity paid him handsomely many years later, for some of the men whose lives he succeeded in saving that day became prominent in the attempt to obtain a pardon for him after he was sentenced to prison in Minnesota for his part in the ill-fated raid on the Northfield Bank.

Thomas Coleman "Cole" Younger, born on 15 January 1844 was the son of Henry Washington Younger, a prosperous farmer from Greenwood, Missouri and Bersheba Leighton Fristoe, daughter of a prominent Jackson County farmer. Cole was the seventh of fourteen children and the eldest brother of Jim, John and Bob Younger. He was an American Confederate guerrilla during the Civil War and later an outlaw with the James-Younger gang. Younger fought as a guerrilla under William Clarke Quantrill. Younger at some point left the bushwhacker ranks and enlisted in the Confederate Army. He was sent to California on a recruiting mission. He returned after the Southern defeat to find Missouri under the rule of a militant faction of Unionists, the Radicals, who soon took over the regular

Republican Party in the state. In the closing days of the war, the Radicals pushed through a new state constitution that barred Confederate sympathizers from voting, serving on juries, holding public office or preaching the gospel from church pulpits.

The southerners were now virtual prisoners in their own homes, the ones who had a home left, with Redlegs and Union militia harassing them as they were criminals.

Chapter 9

By the 2nd day of October, with the gold train robbery coming off without a hitch, the most bountiful haul in the history of outlawry was cached safely in the ore-car unloading, repair barn, and minting facility of Lucky Basin Mine north of Hailey, Idaho. Billy Dunstan and eleven other men with their mounts and forty-two pack mules were awaiting the train's arrival. The thirty men from the train unloaded their mounts, tied them inside the barn, gave them water and hay that was brought in the horse-car with them, and then all forty-two men blew off steam with a cheerful jubilation. While it was still light all the men then pitched in on taking up all the tracks from the railroad to the building. With the help of some mules and rope they dragged the tracks and crossties far out behind the building and covered them in a tailing dump. With shovels found inside the barn they camouflaged the area where the tracks were removed. As they worked on this, Forrest Abernathy and one of his mine workers shower up with a wagon and a team of mules to get another melting pot. A couple of Cole Younger's men helped them remove the melting pot and everything that went with it and put it the wagon. Everyone laid out their bedrolls, got out some beef-jerky and their water bags, chewed on jerky and drink water until they lost the gnawing hunger pains and turned in for the night.

At first light they lead the mules by the gold car and equally divided the gold sacks into their side-bags, and put a few hundred pounds in Forrest's wagon with the melting pot.

"Forrest," Billy asked in the way of a statement. "I assume Captain Frank and Madame La'fay made it back to Timberline."

"Oh Yes Sir, they are workin' at the mine with Pierre. Some of the men are buildin' a corral for the mules on the east side of the building, in back of the horse stalls."

"Horse stalls?" asked Billy.

"Yes Sir, Captain Frank had 50 enclosed stalls built for the hosses. He put 25 on each side of the building, with a steeped roof connecting to the other one."

"Wow, how bout that!" Billy exclaimed. "The Captain thinks of everything. He's got a head on his shoulders."

"By the way," Forrest interjected, directing his question to Billy. "Where in the world did you find the mules."

Billy laughed, "They're Army mules, I borrowed'em from the Fort," he laughed again. "They knowed I'm the Sheriff up at Timberline, and I told'em we brought in a bunch of supplies for the mercantile store and various other businesses for the oncoming winter and I needed some mules to pack'em. I gave'em six quarts of rut-gut whiskey and they told me to help ourselves. We left with'em before daylight. But I'll have to return'em sometime soon."

They all looked disconcerted at Billy, and then at each other to see who might laugh. Cole was the only one to break a laugh.

"I guess you know what you're doin' Billy," Cole said. "I'm sure there are Union troops already scouring the country looking for that train, and you borrow mules from them to transport the gold. But like I said, I'm sure you know what you're doin'."

"They'll never connect it. They have about twice that many mules, and they didn't know how many I took. They were all too drunk to even know when we left. We could keep bout ten of'em and they'd never know the difference. Anyway, damn-it, I had to have some mules."

They left with Forrest leading the way in the wagon, going due east across near the top of the craters where they stopped for the night. They left with the daybreak, intercepting the road to Timberline about mid-day some two days north of Blackfoot. They would spend five more tiring days on the trail prodding along the weary overloaded mules, before taking the old logging road around town and, up to the mine.

The pack mules were put into the new corral while Forrest drove the wagon to the back of the mine building. A number of men helped unload it into the building. When he pulled the wagon back out near the corral, the men brought one mule at a time around the building and into the back where they unloaded the gold sacks into a large pile back of where the new melting pot would go. In a few hours the worn out, unburdened mules, were happy to be given oats and water. Billy told the men to remove all of the pack bags and burn all but five of them.

"I'll need a couple of men to help me return the mules," said Billy.

"I thought," Cole said. "You were going to keep some of them."

"We can't." Billy said. "I would sure like to, but they are all branded with a big U.S. on their rumps. We can't be caught down the line using Union Army mules. We have two of our own and we'll buy another two or three somewhere, or how-ever many we might need. We need to return them late at night so's we can get'em in the corral a'fore they see how many we took, and start to get suspicious."

Billy and three men left the following morning to return the mules to Fort Hall in Blackfoot.

Forrest had lots of help setting the new melting pot. While they were gone Pierre had set up the three ingot stamping presses and one double stamp press for fifty dollar gold pieces. He had stamped a full box of fifty dollar coins and made two buckets of blank planchets for La'fay to start sizing. She told him he needed to find about six or eight more ladies to work as adjusters. He readily agreed with her and asked her if she could find them, while glancing sheepishly at her reaction.

"I'll try," said she.

When the evening supper was finished and the men had started their accustomed discussions, La'fay excused herself pretending to go upstairs. She, with deliberate forethought slipped unseen out the front door and walked hastily up to the saloon. She saw Jake Winston at the bar talking to some men. As she approached him, he saw her and stepped away from the men.

"Mrs. Dunbar," he exclaimed. "I'm pleased to see you, but hardly recognized you. Have you been on the trail?"

"Yes, as a matter of fact, I have. I need to discuss a matter of importance with you."

"Let us have a seat at that far table in the corner—could I get you a drink?"

"No thank you," she said as she went to the table and sat down.

"What could I help you with?" he asked somewhat perplexed as he took his seat.

"It's about the girls that work here.—By the way, where are they tonight?"

"They are not working tonight. In fact they will be off for eight more days by instructions of the doctor."

"Gonorrheal?"

"Yes," he answered, surprised at her shrewd awareness.

"Mister Winston, talk to me about the money. How much does the saloon make from having the girls here, and how much does each individual girl make for herself?"

"That depends on a lot of circumstances. It's hard to put a dollar amount on it because it constantly changes."

"I see, then you don't keep records on the saloon. You can't tell me how much you've made in a month's time or three month's time?"

"No Mam, it don't work that way.

"Well. Mister Winston, it is going to start working that way. Beginning tomorrow, you get a record book and start keeping account of the money you take in daily, and the cost of the operation. You do that or find yourself another job. In the meantime I'm going to talk to the girls about working for awhile in the mine as planchet adjusters. Are the girls upstairs?"

"Yes Mam," Winston answered squeamishly.

La'fay went up the stairs and opened the first door. A girl was sitting up in bed reading a book. La'fay asked her nicely to gather all the girls in her room for a talk.

When the six girls were in the room La'fay told them who she was and found out that they were lucky to make as much as ten dollars a week for themselves. Jake Winston kept most of what they made from the gentlemen callers. She explained to them about the adjuster job and told them they would be paid ten dollars a day for their work. They all were overjoyed to get the positions. La'fay told them to dress warmly without any frills. If they needed to buy shirts and trousers, she told them to go to the mercantile store and charge their purchases to La'fay Dunbar, and it would be wise to get a union suit. "We usually go to the mine after breakfast. We will see you when you can get there. Oh, if you are taking medication from the doctor, bring it with you." La'fay was in her room at the hotel when the miners meeting broke up and welcomed her man with a kiss when he came in.

The following morning at the mine, La'Fay busied herself with setting and calibrating a scale for each of her new employees. She had thought she may have to have the bench lengthened, but was glad to see that there would be enough room for each of the scales and the stamping presses. She then laid out a bunch of fifty dollar planchets in front of every scale along with files and brushes. She looked with admiration on what she had done as Pierre and Frank discreetly observed her.

"Damn-it!" La'fay bellowed. "We need stools. I forgot the stools. We can't all sit on the one stool. Frank, send a couple of men with me to the mercantile store to pack back six stools." Everyone was looking at her but nobody wanted to say anything. Frank motioned for two of the bushwhackers to go with her. Cole Younger and Clell Miller stepped forward.

"Come on Madame La'Fay," said Cole, "me and Clell will go help'ya."

La'fay took three fifty dollar gold pieces from the box, and put them in her pocket. "Let's go," said she, and headed for the door with Cole and Clell following.

"Does anybody know what's goin' on?" asked Frank.

"I wasn't about to ask her," Pierre said. "But I think she's about to hire some adjusters."

They left the mine and went down the road to the mercantile store. Inside, La'fay asked the store manager if the ladies had been in and bought clothes.

"Yes Mam, they sure have. I have their ticket here." He handed it to La'fay. It was for forty-two dollars.

"I also need to buy six stools, about this high." She held her hand out over the floor. The man went over to the side and began to take stools down from a hanging wire that ran across the store. Cole went over and helped him.

"Did the ladies happen to buy hats that they could put their hair up under," asked La'fay.

"No Mam."

"Let me have six hats similar to what I'm wearing."

The manager went and brought back the six western style hats with leather draw strings.

"How much are the stools and hats," asked La'fay.

"The six stools at three dollars is eighteen dollars, and the hats at ten dollars is sixty dollars. Add forty two for the clothes." He was writing it all down. "It all comes to one hundred and twenty dollars."

La'fay handed him the three fifty dollar gold pieces. He gave her back six five dollar greenbacks.

As La'fay, Cole and Clell emerged from the mercantile store, La'fay saw the six girls come out of the saloon.

"Let's hold up a minute," La'fay said. "Those ladies are going with us to the mine."

Cole and Clell with big smiles indicated extreme delight.

"Before you boys get all worked up," La'fay said. "I want you to know they all have gonorrheal.—Cole, you let the other men know."

"Hot-damn," Clell exclaimed. "Is that catchin'?"

"Sure it is," said Cole.

"Well, I sure don't won't to get close to'em," said Clell.

"You can't catch it just getting' close to'em," Cole leaned in close to Clell and whispered in his ear.

"Hot-damn al'mighty!" Clell exclaimed.

La'fay gave each girl a hat and told them to put their hair under it. She then took the stools from Cole and Clell and gave each lady one to pack to the mine.

At the mine La'fay put the ladies through a thorough schooling on how to get the gold planchets ready for stamping.

As Frank and Pierre watched enthusiastically, they glanced at each other. Frank displayed a big smile of proud and loving gratification. As time went by production had increased considerably. Even the mine was producing better as the miners continued to work out the bedrock of the old river channel, and continually wheel-barrowing the larger river rock out of the mine entrance and across about a forty-foot expansion from the horse stalls to the deep ravine running parallel to the building.

Chapter 10

As the first signs of a Timberline winter begin to show its fury with a light snow blowing sideways and biting the face like little flying insects, Frank gave the bushwhackers the option of bunking down in the mine building for the winter or bucking the weather to Blackfoot to catch the train. The Great Northern Flyer ran throughout the winter from Des Moines, through Boise, to Eugene, Oregon as a track running snow-plow proceeded ahead of it. At any rate Frank, so as not to cause awareness, did not want more than four men in any given two weeks going into Blackfoot to catch the train.

Before the snow became too deep, four men who had families in Missouri left the following morning, and four more in two weeks. They each took with them a pouch of six hundred dollars in fifty dollar gold pieces. The remainder of the men stayed for the winter. Most busied themselves helping Forrest in the mine and tending to the horses. Everyone was issued snowshoes to maneuver their way from the hotel to the mine. Food was transported to the mine on a small sleigh pulled by two men with snow-shoes and ropes. Food was mostly always in the way of mulligan and pan bread. Abner kept the fires going and lit the coal-oil stove to warm the mulligan.

President Grant, with his office suffering great injury over the loss of the entire government treasury—and fear of the banking industry shutting down due to its bad debt loss of four billion dollars, had as many as six complete regiments of Union soldiers searching for the mysterious gold train. Adding insult to injury, one regiment of U.S. soldiers was lost to an early morning ambush by Chief Geronimo's Mescalero-Chiricahau Apache warriors in central New Mexico.

By early spring and knowing not in which way to turn, President Grant sent a special envoy to San Antonio to see Captain Barry Battle of the Texas Rangers with the request for the use of his best Ranger as a Presidential U.S. Marshal to conduct a covert investigation on the disappearance of the gold train. His reasoning being that perhaps one good man could better institute ways of tracing the path of the train.

The two distinguished gentlemen introduced themselves as delegates of the President of the United States, and glancing around at the Rangers in the room, asked to speak to him alone. Captain Battle dismissed his men and asked the gentlemen to sit down. They remained standing and explained the President's request.

The first person that came to mind was Junior Barstow. Undoubtedly his best, although he thought for a moment about the displeasure of losing him, he wished to be loyal to the President.

"I have just the man for you, his name is Junior Barstow—shall I have him to come in."

"Please do," said one of the men.

Captain Battle went to the door and told the guard to have Junior Barstow report to his office immediately. The two men then sat down.

Momentarily Junior entered, saluted his Captain and remained at attention.

"At ease, Lieutenant," said the Captain as the two men stood up.

Junior spread his legs and clasped his hands behind his back.

"These two gentlemen are from the President's office in Washington, Captain Battle said. "They wish to borrow a good man to do a job for President Grant. I recommended you. I'll let them tell you about it."

The men introduced themselves as Lester Musgrove, and Henry Arbuckle. Musgrove explained the covert operation as outlined by the President. Arbuckle took a U.S. Marshall badge from his pocket and asked Junior if he would accept the job.

"Sure, if the President needs me, I'm ready to go find his train."

Arbuckle then officially inducted him as a United States Marshall and pinned the badge on his chest, Musgrove took a packet of government script forms from his briefcase and handed them to Junior telling him that he could use them for expenses. They then wished him luck and took their leave.

"Well Captain," Junior said, "I guess I can dig out my civilian suit and leave my uniform in my locker. I probably won't be gone very long. I saw you write their names down, will you give me a copy of them to keep with me?"

They hugged. The Captain choked up, as Junior took the names and went out the door. He took the Ranger saddle off of the red mare and put his own saddle on her, for the first time in three years. She became excited knowing her old saddle was on her. Her skin rippled as she pranced and reared up. "Settle down girl," Junior said, "I've got to go in and change my clothes, then we'll hit the trail." He patted her neck and rubbed her nose to calm her down. Inside the bunk house he got out his black suit, brushed it down and took his off-white hat from the top shelve of the locker. He took his Ranger clothes off including the boots and put his clothes and boots on. After pinning the Marshall badge to his vest and putting his coat and hat on, he admired himself in the mirror, pulling his coat back to expose his badge, he fancied himself as Wyatt Earp, without the mustache, from pictures he had seen of Wyatt's early years as Marshall of Dodge City before going to Tombstone, Arizona.

Junior mounted the red mare and rode a few miles over to where the gold train had been stolen. *"A good place to start,"* he thought. After looking over the first track heading north and seeing that there were no tracks past the stack of crossties, like all of the Union troops, he dismissed it as a likely route for the train. For days he rode the main track west searching for the most likely route. He counted out it going to Mexico. There were no tracks past San Antonio going into Mexico before getting to Tucson, Arizona. The train could only stay on the main track for half a day without making contact with the regular east bound train.

"Alright girl," he said. "We're going back to the second turnoff and give it a more thorough search."

At the second turnoff, Junior dismounted and searched the area for clues. The stack of crossties seemed to have been tampered with. The track under and past them looked as though it had been used. There were boot tracks all around the area. *"These clues could have been purposely made,"* he thought. It all looked to obvious to Junior. He decided to take the first route. *"They could have removed the tracks to throw searchers off. In any case knowing they would have to get away from the main track in a hurry. This would be their best bet,"* was his opinionated conjecture.

Junior again searched the area around the first closed track. *"It's too clean, that means they took this route."* He and the red mare started up the track checking carefully for clues.

For three months Junior followed the railroad track meticulously checking every detail, thinking something like trash or whatever could have been thrown from the train. He carefully followed the track up by Fort Stockton, through Pecos, and into New Mexico. Cool weather was setting in leading up to winter. Junior had stopping along the way to inquire if anyone had heard a locomotive go by.

In Pecos, the man that runs the general mercantile store told him that way back sometime in late last fall his 12 year old son had said that a train came by in the wee hours of the morning. "Everybody said that he must of been dreamin' cause nobody else hear'ed it. The boy would of staked his life on it. He swore he hear'ed it. I'm the only'est one what believed him—cause my boy don't lie." While in Pecos, Junior bought a heavy bearskin coat to suppress the freezing cold and light snow.

During the winter, the people at the mine had stayed busy minting gold coins and ingots. Pierre Beauregard had finished engraving the first ten thousand dollar ingot stamp and they were turning out 23 pound 6 ounce Troy weight gold ingots, like clockwork. The ingots were referred to as "bars", although they were about half the size as a normal gold bullion bar. Pierre worked on the second such stamp. Abner kept all of the stoves and the melting pots burners going to keep the building warm. They all went back and forth to the restaurant wearing snow shoes.

On the face of the Ten Thousand Dollar ingot bar was a line of big trees from one end to the other with a barren mountain rising above them, with the inscription across the top, *The Great Northwest.* Inset across the trees was the word *TIMBERLINE* with the dollar amount of *Ten Thousand Dollars* across the bottom at the base of the trees. The back was left blank except for the mint mark in the center of the bar in small letters that read, *LORI*, an addition which Pierre said was their secret.

The six ladies from the saloon had all worked out great and liked their job of being adjusters. They all talked, as they worked, about plans for a new start when this job played out. None of them wanted to return to the saloon. Alice, one of the ladies, and Clell Miller planned to be married and live in Missouri. Forrest told them that from all indications the jobs would not play out for many years to come.

The devastating winter with its fierce winds and blowing snow in the northeast Texas and southern New Mexico area was more than Junior could take. By the time he reached Carlsbad he was feeling extremely ill, feeling as he may be coming down with consumption. He stopped at the local hotel and rented a room inquiring as to the possibility of a doctor. The hotel manager put him on the first floor, and noticing his feverish condition sent for the doctor.

By the time the doctor arrived Junior had removed his boots and most of his clothes and was lying on the bed shaking with chills. The doctor had the manager send them more quilts to cover Junior. He listened intently to his chest and lungs with his stethoscope. As Junior was shaking uncontrollably and in a state of delirium, the doctor and hotel manager looked through his clothing for identification and found his badge. They didn't find nothing with his name on it but perceived the badge was sufficient to render him the best of treatment. The doctor said they had to reduce his fever, yet keep him warm and bathe his face with cool water. "I'm going to give him something for the fever, and you have someone to stay with him to keep bathing his face, head and neck. I'll come by again about supper time to check on him." The doctor opened his bag and removed a small bottle of liquid opium, put a few drops in a small glass of water. "Ed, help me force this down him."

Ed Waterman, the hotel manager had his daughter, Mary Jane, that worked in the restaurant to stay with Junior and bathe his face to help reduce the fever. Mary Jane was three or four years older than Junior, a somewhat homely woman, not ugly, but also not beautiful. Her pleasing personality gave her an air of amiable respectability. She had lost her husband during the war, fighting for the Union. When Doctor Weathers came back at supper time to see about his patent, Junior was sleeping soundly except for a rumbling in his chest.

"Miss Mary Jane," the doctor said, "His fever has subsided some, but I would like you to remain in his room tonight and make sure his fever doesn't rise, especially to the point of having chills. I will leave another dose of medicine, if he wakes up and becomes irritable, make him take it. And remember the main thing is to not let him get cold."

"Yes Sir, Doctor," she said, "I'll keep him good and warm."

The doctor fixed the medication and said, "I'll be back in the morning, give him this only if he is restless."

"Yes Sir," said she.

Chapter 11

Spring had come and gone by the time Junior left Carlsbad. Mary Jane had been an exceptionally good nurse throughout the winter and spring. He had finally shook the lung and bronchial infection, and made some very good friends, whom he thanked graciously, and paid well with government script.

Some few miles north of Carlsbad the track split, and beings as how the switching implement was set to take the track to the west, so went Junior, being unaware that it was set that way purposely after the gold train went by it. In ten days time Junior had followed the wrong track around the base of a mountain and into a canyon with rugged boulders on either side. After a considerable way through the canyon he began to hear the sound of whooping, yelling, and rifle shots. He prodded the red mare to quickly move into the rocks. As he maneuvered through the big rocks closer to the commotion he saw a troop of Union soldiers in confrontation with a small band of Mescalero Apaches that had attacked two farm wagons, adapted to the use as covered wagons, and headed west through the valley. Some of the Indians had cut loose the two-up teams and taken them up a draw toward the north mountains. By the time the soldiers had spotted them, the Indians had already killed four people, looted, and fired the wagons.

The red mare became tense, trembled and bolted back as a warning to Junior. Junior quickly drew one of his revolvers as he glimpsed a movement through the crevice of two boulders. He heard sobbing as he dismounted and cautiously proceeded to move around one of the boulders. His mind stunned momentarily as he saw a little yellow-haired girl, squatted down sobbing and staring frightfully up at him through wide misty blue eyes. As his senses quickly returned, he saw that it was not a little girl at all, but a beautiful full grown young lady.

Junior holstered his pistol, took out a bandana from his pocket and slowly in a consoling manner reached over and dabbed her tear stained face.

"You aren't hurt, are you?" asked he.

"No, I'm scared," her soft voice trembled.

Junior had noticed that she wore a large man's shirt, with the sleeves turned up. Also, she wore men's pants rolled up, with a cotton rope for a belt, and overly large brogans. He removed his black suit coat and placed it around her shoulders.

"What's your name?" asked Junior.

"Susan," she said, gazing wide-eyed into his eyes. "Mary Susan Spencer."

"My name is Junior, where did you manage to find these clothes?"

"They belong to my uncle," said she, glibly.

Junior backed up so as to see the soldiers. They were digging graves for the dead travelers. He went back to where Susan was.

"Do you feel like standing up?" asked he.

"Yes, I'll try," replied Susan, as she slowly stood and continued to weep.

"They are burying your people out there. We must go out and let them know what to put on the markers." He wiped her face again, and put his arm around her shoulders. He led the red mare as they slowly walked out to the soldiers.

"Hello there," said a soldier, as he approached them. "My name is Sanders,—Lieutenant Sanders, Are you part of this party?"

"Yes, this young lady is, I found her in the rocks. I heard the commotion and worked my way up through the boulders where I discovered her," said Junior.

"Mam," asked Sanders. "Are the deceased akin to you?"

"Yes, my grand-parents, and my aunt and uncle," said she.

"Your parents weren't along?" asked Spencer.

"No," I lost my parents back in Missouri, We were on our way to California."

"Where in Missouri?" asked Junior.

"We had a farm near Glasgow. It was burned by Redlegs. My mother and daddy, and my big brother was all killed—I was off pickin' blackberries when it happened. I saw 'em from a distance and hid in the woods. My aunt and uncle, and my grand-parents who lived with them , were going to California, a'fore they too were burned out, so I come with 'em."

"Lieutenant," called a soldier. "We're ready to cover 'em up!"

"Yes corporal, carry on,—Mam, I would rather you not view them, It would not be a pleasant sight. I took the identifications from the two men. I will register them as deceased in the Lincoln courthouse."

"Okay, thank you," said she.

"Sir," Sanders directed his speech to Junior. "I will take control of the girl, and try to find her a home in Lincoln."

"The girl stays with me," said Junior, as he took his badge from his vest pocket and pinned it on his vest.

"But Sir," Sanders said. "It's my duty to—"

"It's your duty to do what I tell you to do," said Junior, as he turned to face him, revealing the Marshall's badge.

"Yes Sir," said Sanders. "I didn't know. Yes Sir, you keep the girl."

"Aren't you supposed to be searching for a gold train?" asked Junior.

Sanders scrutinized Junior momentarily before yelling at his men to mount up. Susan moved over beside Junior, put her arm around him, kissed him on the cheek, and thanked him.

Being from Glasgow, Junior figured that she was like family. "Tell me about your family. Did ya'll know the James boys?"

"My daddy, and especially my brother knew'em well. I've seen'em before at our house, but I never really talked to'em."

"I'll get on the mare. You put your foot in the stirrup, hold on to me, and swing up behind me onto my bedroll."

They left with Susan holding on to Junior with her arms around him. They followed the railroad track for a few hours until it emptied into a vast rolling prairie. In the far distance they could make out a town with the railroad track headed straight to it.

"You ain't go'na leave me in that town, are'ya?" Susan asked. "I don't wont'ya to leave me, Junior. I won't ta'stay with you."

Junior favored a considerable joy in his heart, and threw reason to the wind. Against what should be his better judgment, he knew he would let her stay with him.

In the town of Lincoln, Junior had Susan outfitted with rawhide riding pants and coat, boots, a hat, and told her to get a warm shirt and some under-things, They then went to the local hotel where he told the proprietor to have a bath poured for the lady in their best room. He left her there and went shopping for a good horse, complete with saddle, saddle-bags and a bedroll. He then bought a new model Colt six-shooter with holster, and told the man he would bring a lady in for the belt adjustment. Junior was like a kid in a candy store, marveling at the thought of keeping her with him. He was tired of being alone, and anyway he already concluded that she was almost family.

Come morning he picked her up looking ecstatically marvelous in her new clothes. They picked up her horse, a sleek muscular buckskin gelding, and had the gun-belt adjusted to fit her. Junior paid for everything with government script, and they continued to follow the railroad track as it turned slightly northeast straight into the open desert.

The trouble with Timberline was that it was too far off the beaten path. Most of the bushwhackers had left, four at a time. Only Cole Younger, and Clell Miller were left at the mine. The men were constantly picking big nuggets from the sluice box. The placer gold off the old river bedrock was more than could be hoped for. Everyone was happily working hard at striking fifty dollar gold coins and Forrest was stamping ten thousand dollar ingot bars with two presses while Pierre worked at engraving a third ingot stamp.

Wooden boxes had been built to pack the ingot bars. Ten to the box weighed 236 pounds Troy weight which could be handled sufficiently by two strong men. Sixty box's at the price per ounce of gold being $70. as set in California, were valued at $100,083,600. So one of the 60 boxes would have only 5 bars in it to make the weight right for 100 million dollars, and the crew was working on the second 60 box's. The League of Rebel Insurrectionist was well on their way. Another six months will give them another 100 million dollars. Another year with no unforeseen problems will double that amount, but now with 100 million it was time to go to Washington and start negotiating the rebirth of the South.

Junior wasn't in any hurry to get anywhere fast. He told Susan about Grant's missing gold train, and how he had been commissioned to try to find it.

"You ain't no Yankee, are you?" she looked questioningly at him with a hint of worry in her big beautiful blue eyes.

"No Susan, I ain't no Yankee. He then told her the whole story of changing his name. Riding with Bill Anderson and Archie Clements, and how he was good friends with Frank and Jesse. She leaned over in her saddle and kissed him on the cheek.

"I'm glad," she said. "I don't think I could ever love a Yankee."

"Well, I'm sure glad I'm not a Yankee," said he.

"Me too, cause I'm already planning some day to marry you."

That came as such a shock Junior became embarrassingly flustered and changed the subject. He spoke to her without looking, because he knew his face was reddened.

"Susan, do you know how to shoot that pistol?"

"Sure," she answered. We had guns around the house since I was a little kid. Orville, my brother taught me how to shoot at an early age."

"*Orville,—Orville Spencer,*" Junior recalled silently. "*I remember him, he was at Lawrence, Kansas with Quantrill, when I was there with Anderson, somewhat older than me, but nonetheless I remember him.*"

"Let us stop up the way by that stand of cottonwood and do a little target practice, I want to see how good you are. With the cottonwoods there should be some water there too," said he.

There was indeed a spring fed pool. The water ran off some forty feet and disappeared into the ground. From the tracks, it seemed to be a favorite watering hole for the multitude of desert animals, and probably Indians.

"Let's go on further, there's no telling what or who is watching us," Junior said. "Let's not linger here."

They laid the reins across their horse's necks, turned and rode away at a trot. About forty miles further into a picturesque mesa with steep flat topped buttes scattered in every direction, the railroad track came to an end. Junior was flabbergasted. He got off the red mare and walked around. Susan said nothing, she only watched him. It just ended with no sign of it ever having continued. After carefully remembering when the track split, he knew he took the track to the west. So he must go east to find the other track. "*Now that was quite a ploy,*" he thought to himself, to throw me off. "*So, that means the gold train had to take that other track. We'll have to go east till we pick it up."*

Junior took a compass from his saddlebag, looked at it, mounted the red mare and motioned for Susan. They headed across the mesa going due east. *"I'll explain it all to her later,"* thought Junior.

"You better look for a good place to stop for the night," Susan called to Junior. "It will soon be dark." In the distance, Junior had already spotted a dense thicket of Mesquite trees. "We'll camp up ahead yonder in that Mesquite," said he.

They found an open area inside the thicket where they unsaddled and tethered the horses. They were rolling out their bedrolls when Susan said something about making coffee.

"Dark is setting in," Junior said, "We can't have a fire. It would illuminate our bedroom and the Indians could see what we're doing." Susan crouched on her knees and stared precariously at Junior. She stammered hesitantly, "what do you mean—see what we're doing?—all we'll be doin' is sleepin," she articulated haughtily.

"So go to sleep—there's some jerky in my saddlebag, if'n you're hungry," said he.

"Hrumphh," grunted Susan, as she flopped down and pulled a blanket over her head.

Chapter 12

The sun was high the next day when Junior decided to stop and see how well Susan could shoot. It had weighed heavy on his mind, for he feared they may encounter Indians. He reigned up near some cacti with blooms on the pads. He motioned for her to dismount. She pulled on up closer to him and did so.

"You see those buds on the cacti pads, out yonder?"

"Yes."

"From here, let me see you shoot one off."

She pulled the six-shooter and looked it over. "I would do better with one of your ball and cap Navy Colts," she said. "That's the only kind of pistol I've ever shot."

He handed her his left hand pistol and took hers. He watched her as she looked it over and weighed it in her hand for balance. Junior half laughed, wondering if this bit of a girl could even hold this heavy pistol out straight to shoot it. She walked back, handed him her horses reins to hold. Stepped out a ways, half crouched and shot three quick consecutive shots from the hip. She turned a complete circle while moving over, and shot three more buds from the next cacti plant. She pulled the cylinder pin and handed him the spent cylinder. "Give me another cylinder," said she.

Junior took the pistol from her and replaced the cylinder. He put her other pistol and the spent cylinder in his saddleback, and handed her back the Navy colt.

"Here, you keep this'un," he said, with a slight feeling of stupidity, "I have two more in my saddlebag. Don't shoot no more, it's a waste of lead. Your brother taught you well.—I wouldn't want to get in no gunfight with'ya. Let's keep goin', maybe we'll come to a town before dark, where we can get something good to eat."

"I sure hope so, I'm starvin'." answered Susan as she holstered the Navy colt and mounted the buckskin. Junior mounted the red mare, and they continued east in a soft trot.

In two days of intermittently walking and trotting the horses, they came upon the railroad track. In the distance looking north they could make out the form of a town. The closer they came, the smaller the town looked. As they slowly walked the horses into town, they saw a saloon/café sign on the first building. There was a livery, a Sheriff's office, a mercantile store and the Mescal Town Hall that also accommodated the Mayor's office and the Justice of the Peace. Scattered around town were a few resident houses. They rode to the end of town, turned around and went back to the saloon/café.

Inside the door they saw four gun toting drifter type cowboys standing at the bar, and a man wiping the bar. They went to the far table and sat down. Junior could not help but see the men at the bar eye-balling them as they went to sit down. The man wiping the bar came over to the table.

"Evenin' folks, what would be yer pleasure?"

"We're lookin' for somethin'ta' eat," said Junior.

"We don't have a regular menu," said the man. "But my wife can fix'ya up with two nice steaks."

"How is that with you, Susan?"

"That would be great by me," said she, with a pleasing smile.

"Al'right Sir, two steaks it'll be," said Junior.

"Two steaks it'll be," repeated the man as he went to the kitchen.

One of the men from the bar, wearing a malicious smile, sauntered over close to the table.

"Is you two youngster's just'a passin' through town?"

"Yes," said Junior. "And we don't need any company."

"Ya'don't have'ta get huffy. I just wanted ta'say how pretty y'all was. Specially this little yeller haired female." He reached over toward Susan's hair. Junior came out of his chair with his gun drawn and cracked the man against the side of his head with it. The man went down as Susan, like a striking snake, came out of her chair with gun drawn covering the others at the bar, as they were in the process of drawing their guns. One had his gun out and bringing it up. All in a split second, Susan had dropped him with a ball to his chest. The other two left their guns holstered and raised their hands.

On hearing the pistol shot, someone from the kitchen ran to get the sheriff. He was there momentarily, along with another man. Junior had unbuttoned his coat revealing the badge pinned on his vest. He explained in detail what had happened. The sheriff handcuffed the groggy man as he was coming to, and took him and the other two to jail. He and his man returned to take away the dead man, and told Junior and Susan to enjoy their steaks, and don't worry about the men getting out of jail anytime soon.

JIM FEAZELL

When the proprietor's wife, brought the steaks out, Junior was surprised to see that she was an Indian squaw. The man noticing Junior's surprise, told him his wife was Mescalero. "She's a very loving woman and faithful wife. Also, her living here is the reason this town is still here. She is the eldest daughter of Red Cloud, who is one of Chief Geronimo's lieutenant's. Susan was astounded to think that this beautiful woman was the daughter of an Indian warrior. She had never seen an Indian squaw before, and was taken aback by her beauty.

Junior's mind was working a mile a minute as he ate his steak. He knew he had only known Susan but a short time, and he also knew he had grown to love her. Without taking anything for granted, he believed in all his heart that she loved him, and he thought this was the perfect time to pop the question. Anyway, he kept remembering that she had said someday she was going to marry him. He didn't want to screw this up, he wanted to do it right. "*So,*" he thought, "*just leave reason aside and do it right.*" He wiped his mouth, laid the napkin on his plate, got up and went around the table, kneeled down and took Susan's hand in his. "Susan," he said. "I know I've been an ass, but darlin' I love you with all my heart—will you marry me?"

Although, surprised out of her wits, Susan was overcome with joy. She got up from the chair, pulled him to his feet, and kissed him long and hard. "There is a Justice of the Peace down the road," said she.

Overheard by the proprietor, he approached them and happily said,

"I have an upstairs room for you, my friends. You are welcome to it for the night, with no charge."

"Thank you, we will be right back," said Junior.

As it was still daylight, they walked down to the town hall and enquired after the Justice of the Peace. He, an elderly man, married them, recorded it, and gave Susan the marriage certificate, stating the names as Franklin Dunbar Junior, and Mary Susan Spencer, married on May 9th, 1875.

They took their saddlebags as the saloon proprietor stabled their horses at the livery and showed them to their room.

"Susan baby," he said, "I noticed when you shot the man, that you didn't aim. Do you always shoot that way?"

"Yeah, I aimed Junior. I aimed before I drew my pistol."

"Oh, okay—damn, I love you."

Late on the following morning, the newly-weds happily set out following the railroad track north watching for clues of any kind. Susan rode up close by him, occasionally goading him with sensual inclinations, to stop for awhile. It took only a small bit of her provocations to remind him that they had only this past night gotten married. With nothing but jack-rabbits and possibly a deer or two to see them, they stopped in the shade of a small clump of mesquite. As they would be spending their honeymoon traveling horseback through the southwestern desert, it stood to reason that they would take considerable time getting from the small town of Mescal to Santa Rosa, where the railroad track turned directly west to Tijeras, and northwest to Farmington before entering Utah.

Even though they traveled the desert horseback for their bed of roses honeymoon, Junior and Susan immensely relished the happiness they shared. He still maintained a loyalty to his sworn duty, and carefully watched the track dump on both sides for even the slightest clue to the probability of the whereabouts of the missing gold train.

It would have to be termed an audacious irony to think that a rebel bushwhacker would be commissioned indirectly by the President of the United States to try to find his stolen gold, and even more ironical to think that this rebel bushwhacker's own father would be the one that stole the gold. Should Junior happen to trace the gold to the Timberline mine, what with his devotion to his newfound occupation, where would his loyalty lie?

A distinguishing characteristic in the Grant Presidency was his concern with the plight of African Americans and native Indian tribes, in addition to civil rights for all Americans. Grant's 1868 campaign slogan, "Let us have peace," defined his motivation and assured his success. As president for two terms, Grant made many advances in civil and human rights. In 1869 and 1871, he signed bills promoting black voting rights and prosecuting Klan leaders. He won passage of the Fifteenth Amendment, which gave freedmen the vote, and the KKK Act, which empowered the president "to arrest and break up disguised night marauders.

Grant presided over the last half of Reconstruction. He supported amnesty for former Confederates and signed the Amnesty Act of 1872 to further this. He favored a limited number of troops to be stationed in the South—sufficient numbers to protect Southern Freedmen, suppress the violent tactics of the KKK, and prop up Republican Governors, but not so many as to create resentment in the general population. President Grant had signed the Naturalization

Act of 1870 that allowed persons of African descent to become citizens of the United States.

Taking a look back at President Grant. During the Mexican American War (1846-1848), Lieutenant Grant served under Generals Zachary Taylor and Winfield Scott. Although assigned as a quartermaster, he got close enough to the front lines to see action, participating in the battles of Resaca de la Palma, Palo Alto, Monterrey, and Veracruz. At Monterrey, he carried a dispatch voluntarily on horseback through a sniper-lined street. He was twice brevetted for bravery: at Molino del Rey and Chapultepec. He was a remarkably close observer of the war, learning to judge the actions of colonels and generals, particularly admiring how Zachary Taylor campaigned. At the time he felt that the war was a wrongful one and believed that territorial gains were designed to spread slavery throughout the nation, writing in 1883, "I was bitterly opposed to the measure, and to this day, regard the war, which resulted, as one of the most unjust ever waged by a stronger against a weaker nation".

On August 22, 1848, Grant married Julia Boggs Dent, the daughter of a prominent Missouri slave plantation family. Together, they had four children: Frederick Dent Grant; Ulysses S. "Buck" Grant, Jr.; Ellen Wrenshall "Nellie" Grant; and Jesse Root Grant.

Lieutenant Grant remained in the army and was assigned to several different posts. He was sent west to Fort Vancouver in the Oregon Territory in 1852, initially landing in San Francisco during the height of the California Gold Rush. Julia was eight months pregnant with their child and could not accompany him because a lieutenant's salary, at the time, would not support a family on the frontier. The journey proved to be a horrid ordeal and Grant narrowly escaped a cholera epidemic while traveling overland through Panama. Grant set up both a ship and a tent hospital in Cruces to take care of the sick soldiers. There were 150 4th Infantry fatalities. After Grant arrived in San Francisco he was stationed in the Pacific Northwest. At Fort Vancouver, he served as Quartermaster of the 4th Infantry Regiment. Grant came in contact with western American Indian tribes. In 1853, Grant stated that the Native Americans were "harmless" and that they would be "peaceful" had they not been "put upon by the whites". He stated that the Klickitat tribe was formerly "powerful", yet had been inundated by white civilizations "whiskey and Small pox."

In 1854, he was promoted to captain, one of only fifty still on active duty, and assigned to command Company F, 4th Infantry, at Humboldt, on the northwest California coast. Without explanation, he abruptly resigned from the Army with little notice on July 31, 1854. The commanding officer at Fort Humboldt, Bvt. Lt. Col. Robert C. Buchanan, a strict disciplinarian, learned that Grant was intoxicated off duty while seated at the pay officers table. Buchanan had previously warned Grant several times to stop binge drinking. Rather than court-martial, Buchanan gave Grant an ultimatum to sign a drafted resignation letter. Grant resigned; the war department stated on his record, "Nothing stands against his good name". Rumors, however, persisted in the regular army of Grant's intemperance.

A civilian at age 32, Grant struggled through seven financially lean years. From 1854 to 1858, he labored on a family farm near St. Louis, Missouri, using slaves owned by Julia's father, but it did not prosper. In 1856, Grant, in order to give his family a home, made a house he called

"Hardscrabble." Julia, however, did not like the house, what she described as an "unattractive cabin." In 1858, Grant bought a slave from Julia's father, which made him one of twelve U.S. Presidents who owned slaves during their lifetime. From 1858 to 1859, he was a bill collector in St Louis. In 1860, after many failed business pursuits, he was given a job as an assistant in his father's tannery in Galena, Illinois. The leather shop, "Grant & Perkins", sold harnesses, saddles, and other leather goods and purchased hides from farmers in the prosperous Galena area. He moved his family to Galena before the Civil War broke out.

Up until the outbreak of the Civil War, Grant kept any political opinions private and never endorsed any candidate running for public office. He also, at this time had no animosity toward slavery. His father-in-law was a prominent Democrat in St. Louis, a fact that contributed to a failed attempt to become county engineer in 1859. In the 1856 presidential election, he voted for the Democratic candidate James Buchanan to prevent secession and because "I knew Fremont," the Republican presidential candidate. In 1860, he favored Democratic presidential candidate Stephen A Douglas over Abraham Lincoln, but did not vote. His own father was a prominent Republican in Galena. It was during the Civil War that his political sympathies coincided with the Republicans' aggressive prosecution of the war. In 1864, his patron Congressman Elihu B. Washburne used Grant's private letters as campaign literature for Lincoln's reelection. In 1868, Grant, affiliated with the Radical Republicans, was nominated as the Republican presidential candidate.

Chapter 13

Susan was first to notice the serene boulder strewn area shaded by a high plateau setting about a mile down a descending valley slope.

"Look down yonder, Junior," she said excitedly.

"The shade sure looks invitin'," he said, "let's go check it out."

They rode into the shade for quite a ways before reaching the huge boulders and ragged rock formations from the bottom skirt of the plateau. As they rode on encircling the plateau, there suddenly appeared an abundance of cottonwood trees alining the banks of a spring fed stream. The stream bubbled up from the ground into a large pool and flowed over and around big rocks for about two hundred feet before it disappeared into the ground. They, looking excitedly at one another, quickly dismounted and led their horses to the edge of the water and let them drink their fill.

Junior led the horses back away from the stream, tethered them, loosened the saddle cinches, and broke off two limbs of leaves from a tree for them to eat. While Junior did this, Susan laid out her bedroll, pulled off her boots, stripped off her clothes and jumped wildly into the spring. She surfaced with her mouth open trying to scream, but no sound came out, the water was so cold it had robbed her of breath. By the time she did scream, Junior had stripped, gotten a bar of lie soap from his saddlebag and jumped in. They both splashed around screaming. Junior tried to lather the soap with no luck. They climbed out and shared Susan's towel from her bedroll. Shivering and teeth chattering they quickly began to get back into their clothes to help themselves get warm when Junior spotted a band of about thirty Indian warriors headed across the plain toward where they were.

"Darling," he said. "Don't get excited, but get your clothes and boots on as quickly as possible. There are Indians headed toward us." He got into his clothes and boots in record time, strapped on his guns, cinched up the saddles, and removed the tethers. Susan balled up her half wet hair and put on her hat, before strapping on her gunbelt.

The Indians had spotted them and were riding hard toward them, yelping like scalded coyotes.

"Leave the bedroll," Junior excitedly exclaimed, "Let's go!"

They swung into their saddles and headed down and across the stream coming dangerously close at an angle to the Indians. Before they could get to navigable ground for running, two of the lead Indians were grabbing for the buckskins halter. Susan pulled her Navy Colt and shot both of them from their ponies. Junior shot the next closest two. Had he tried to shoot the two trying to stop the buckskin, Susan would have been in his line of fire. They reached open range and begin pulling away from the Indians. Their one salvation was that these Indians only had bows and arrows, and spears. Had they of had rifles it would have been curtains for Junior and Susan.

As the Indians still pursued Junior and Susan, the U.S. cavalry showed up for the rescue with the "bugler" blowing charge and the "stars and stripes" flying. The cavalry rode toward and by Junior and Susan, and intercepted the renegade Indians. Most of the Indians were killed, but a few got away.

The Captain of the Union Army troop told Junior and Susan that the renegades were part of Chief Ouray's tribe of the Southern Ute Indians. "After the Black Hawk War of 1865", he said, "The army had coerced the Ute's to relocate to reservations, and since then Chief Ouray has had trouble controlling the tribe's braves. All the young bucks want to do is fight, and consequently there are skirmishes constantly breaking out. Before the Black Hawk War, the Ute's had fought with the U.S. Army against the Apache."

"Junior," Susan said sheepishly, "when we get back to the railroad track, let's not stray from it until we find a town to get a hot bath and a soft bed."

"I'll go for that." said he.

Early summer saw most of the snow gone from Timberline, leaving the town looking like a gigantic hog-wallow. Throughout the winter and a rapidly thawing spring, the minting of coins and bars at the Timberline mine never slowed down. At one point, however, it had gotten so frigid most of the people had decided not to make the trip to town at night, but instead to stay at the mine. The ladies all had brought bedrolls and extra covering to the mine and put it all on the other side of the room from the men. The restaurant sent ample food for everyone.

Seeing that Clell and Alice had moved to an inconspicuous bedding place, it wasn't long unto Cole and the miners were also bedding subtly with a lady. Reason being, they said, that body heat is advantageously superior to clothing.

Wondering how the placer miners around the mountain had wintered. Frank decided to go see. He had never been around to see them. He had only seen groups of them at various times making the walk, where they intercepted the trail coming from the back of town, to the water wagon in town, and going back with buckets of water to use in their rockers and small sluices. He walked about two miles following their path up and around to where he intercepted a ledge on the side of a long crevice that opened some forty feet down into the rock. The crevice, about fifty feet wide had exposed the old river bed around the mountain some two or three miles from the Timberline mine. At a place where the ledge widened out and the cliff gave back, affording room for the miners to erect forty or so small tents to sleep in, they had made ladders from pine saplings brought up from the forest. They used the ladders to descend the crevice wall. There were also numerous holes picked into the flat rock area among the tents to use for fire-pits to cook over. It was alike unto itself, a small mining town. Frank stopped and talked to a miner working on his home-made rocker/shaker that is used for washing the gravel to loosen it from the gold, so it can be separated. He could see, he estimated, about forty men working at the bottom of the crevice. He could also see that they were laying aside large piles of river-rock and working in the holes.

"Hi friend," Frank said. "Looks like y'all made it through the rough winter."

"We lost eight men from the cold, and the sickness what come'd with it. Some of the men buried'em down yonder where the ground softens at th'bottom of th'dome along with three others what had already died."

"Sorry to hear that—is this strike paying off, for'ya?"

"Not so's we can brag bout it. Some days it's pretty good, others it ain't so good. I hear tell y'alls hard-rock mine is doing good."

"Not too bad.—You know me, do'ya?"

"Yes Sir, ever'body knows you. We see'ya some time's when we're in town fer supplies. You're Captain Frank.

"Do you know Forrest Abernathy?"

"I've heared of'em—don't know'em directly. He's yer boss man at th'mine, ain't he?"

"Yeah, my wife and I will be leaving sometime soon. Could be that Forrest will be looking for a few trustworthy workers. If'n you know of any such people, he pay's ten dollars a day."

"Ceptin' fer me and my brother, Jim, I don't know off-hand of any such men. Not up here anyhow, nothing but no-good rapscallion's up here. Fact is, there is talk amongst some of probably robbin' y'all. Me and Jim, my brother, might be interested though. We sure ain't making that much here. Just keep thinking we might hit a good hole. My name's Wilber Clapton, that'll be Wilber and Jim. Tell'em we'll be more'n probably come'n ta'see'em."

"Okay Wilber, I'll tell Forrest y'all might come by ta'see'em."

"Yeah, we might just do that, Captain."

On returning to the mine, the first thing Frank did was tell Forrest of his trip, and about Wilber and Jim Clapton.

"Yeah Captain," Forrest said. "I've been around there to see if their diggin's might have any interference with y'alls mine. I couldn't see any that I could tell. They are up on top of the river bed. They won't never hit bedrock cause they ain't got enough room to put the tailin's. Could be that we could use the brothers, once you and th'Misses have left. In the meantime I think we best hire two more guards to work with the two we have, and let them know of the robbery talk. I also checked with the land office to see if they had legitimate claims. The man at the office said it was one consolidated claim with more than fifty names on it. He said, yes, it was legitimate.

Captain Frank, Madame La'fay, Pierre Beauregard, Forrest Abernathy, and Sheriff Billy Dunstan sat in the Hotel restaurant following a late supper and having coffee as they contemplated plans for shipping the first 100 million, which will be in 60 boxes.

"It is my contention," said Captain Frank, "that when we ship it, we should wait until an agreement has been finalized with Grant, and ship it directly to Washington."

"I definitely agree with you," said Pierre, "we sure wouldn't want a boxcar of gold side-tracked in Missouri awaiting a decision."

"I've already been calculating gittin' the gold to the train at Blackfoot," Billy said. "We can take all sixty boxes in two sturdy wagons with four-up teams. I would suggest four heavily armed guards. I will go as one of them, and make arrangements for some of the Union soldiers at the Fort to assist in loading the gold into the boxcar. As a matter of fact I bet we could, with Presidential approval, borrow a few soldiers from the Fort as guards all the way to Washington."

"Captain," asked Forrest, "When do you and the Madam expect to be leaving?"

"Most any day now, I should get started on gleaning my intelligence task, or I might say—testin' the waters. But then, on the other hand, I'm thinking of waiting till we evaluate and resolve this robbery rumor. It was said by Wilber as hearsay which he didn't elaborate on, so I do need to ask him more about it. I can't visualize any of that bunch conducting a robbery up here where they wouldn't have any kind of a chance of making a clean getaway. Hell, I don't think any of them even has a hoss. The only hosses at the livery stable are ours, Pierre's, and Billy's. I was in there early this morning checking on them."

"Yeah," Billy said, "probably someone just flappin' his tongue cause he's irritated with the reality of deprivation. As you said Captain, a closer talk with Wilber will probably bear that out.—By the way, after you left this mornin' I took my hoss to the mine and stabled him there."

"Billy," La'fay asked, "Do you have to make arrangements for a boxcar in Blackfoot, or do they always have one available?"

"Yeah, I'll send someone well in advance to get the depot agent to have us one assigned and put on the sidetrack, plus a horse car."

"Listen y'all," Forrest said, as he got up, straightened his suspenders and put on his coat. "I'm going back up to th'mine and stay the night with Cole and them. I'm still a bit concerned about that robbery talk."

"Hold up Forrest," Billy said, "I'll go with you."

"Not me," Pierre said, "I'm goin' up to bed. I'm tired."

"Yeah," La'fay said. "It's been a long day. Let's go to bed, Captain."

Grant's inability to establish personal accountability among his subordinates and cabinet members was what brought on the many scandals during his administration. Grant often attacked vigorously when critics complained, being protective of his subordinates. Although personally honest with money matters, Grant was weak in his selection of subordinates, often favoring military associates from the war over talented and experienced politicians. He also protected close friends with his Presidential power and pardoned several convicted officials after they had served only a few months in prison. His failure to establish working political alliances in Congress allowed the scandals to spin out of control. At the conclusion of his second term, Grant wrote to Congress that, "Failures have been errors of judgment, not of intent." Nepotism was rampant. Around 40 family relatives financially prospered while Grant was President.

There were 11 scandals directly associated with Grant's two terms as President of the United States. The main scandals included Black Friday in 1869 and the Whiskey Ring in 1875. The primary instigator and contributor to many of these scandals was Grant's personal secretary, Orville E. Babcock, who indirectly controlled many cabinet departments and was able to delay investigations by reformers. Babcock had direct access to Grant at the White House and had tremendous influence over who could see the President.

Grant appointed Benjamin Bristow to the Secretary of Treasury in 1874, who uncovered and shut down the notorious Whiskey Ring. When Secretary Bristow discovered that the President's personal secretary Babcock was involved in the ring, Grant became defensive. Grant eventually defended Babcock in an unprecedented 1875 deposition during the Whiskey Ring graft trials. The result of Grant's deposition saved his friend Babcock with an acquittal. However, political enemies, and the unpopularity of giving the deposition for Babcock, and although not a scandal, but the loss of what became known by constituencies as "Grant's gold," ruined any chances for Grant getting a third term nomination.

Junior, seeing that the track was open to by-pass Santa Rosa took the spur toward town.

"We goin' to town are we?" asked Susan.

"I thought we'd get something good to eat, and maybe a room for the night with that hot bath, if'n all seems peaceable."

Susan was immediately exhilarated. "Hot diggity-dog!!" she exclaimed loudly, "a bed, a nice clean bed!"

"If there's one to be had in town, we'll certainly get it."

"I hope there is, it will sure beat them cold rivers—and specially the springs."

"Yep, it sure will," Junior laughed.

Chapter 14

Like most towns of reasonable size, they spotted a restaurant/hotel about mid-way of the main street. There was a general store across from the restaurant, and a livery down the street from it, after passing one of the four visible saloons. There was a most valuable thing missing from this mix. "People," there were no people. Junior had discerned that Santa Rosa had to have been a cattle town before the railroad shut down. On the way in he had seen a bunch of holding pens along the railroad track. They hitched the horses in front of the restaurant, and went inside.

"Hi strangers," was the friendly greeting from the lady at the register. "Y'all look like you're probably hungry."

"Yes Mam," Junior said. "Where is everybody?—the place looks like a ghost town."

"Most of the men folk," she said, "are on a cattle drive."

"Yeah," said Junior, "I guess that is the only way to get the cattle to market, what with the railroads shut down. Where are they taking them?"

"Their going east, bearing to the south," she said, "to Fort Worth, Texas. What would y'all like to eat?"

"I'd like a steak," Susan said, "real well done. "What about you darling, do you want a steak?"

"Sure," said Junior.

"Then we'll need a room, and a tub of hot water," said Susan.

"Can you handle all of that, Mam?" asked Junior.

"Yeah," the lady said, "I have help in the back, I'll go get the bath started and put on the steaks."

"Before you do that, I need to find out if you have any objection to taking government script for payment." He took his badge from his vest pocket and laid it on the table.

"You're a government Marshal?"

"Yes Mam," said Junior, "I'm a special Marshall for President Grant."

"And I'm his deputy," quipped Susan.

"She's pullin' your leg, Mam. She's my wife."

"I don't have any script forms," the lady said, "But we can write something out to approximate one. I'm sure that will work with your signature on it."

"I have some in my saddlebag." Junior said, "I'll take the hosses over to the livery and bring one back with me."

When Junior returned with his saddlebags the steaks were ready. He took a script form from his saddlebag and gave it to the lady.

"I'll add the livery fee to your bill, my husband owns it, but he's on the cattle drive."

"He also raises cattle?"

"He has about three hundred head on the drive. The two biggest ranchers in the valley set up the drive, and invited all the small ranchers to join in with their cattle. They are taking something in excess of four thousand head. Lester, my husband said the only way to get them to the stock pens in Fort Worth is to drive them. God help us, I hope it don't take all the year, I'm missing him something terrible already.—Oh, my name is Mary, so you don't have to keep saying Mam."

"My name is Mary too," Susan said. "Mary Susan. My husband's name is Frank Junior. He's named after his daddy."

Captain Frank jumped out of bed to the loud knocking on his hotel room door. Before opening the door he asked through it, who is knocking as he stood to the side as a precaution.

"It's Billy," came the reply. "Open up—hurry!"

Captain Frank opened the door. Billy did not attempt to come in. He stood in the hall and talked with a high pitch, inspired with enthusiasm.

"Captain, the robbers are go'na strike sometime in the early hours of the morning. We must all be ready for them. Wilber and Jim came to the mine to warn you. They got there bout the same time as me," Billy said, "we will take the fight to them on the outside, and keep them from coming in, so's the ladies won't get hurt. Cole, Clell, Forrest, and the guards are getting' ready fer'em. I'll go down and saddle yer hoss while'st you get yer clothes on. Oh, Wilber said they wudn't planin' no get-a-way, they's planin' to kill us all and bury us. Then, he said they was goin' to bury our gold till they could slip it out of town. You can wake up Pierre if'n you want to, or just let him sleep. I don't know if'n he even has a gun, or not."

As Frank shut the door, La'fay hurriedly got up and began to get dressed.

"You don't have to go Baby-doll, lessen you just want to," said Frank as he pulled on his pants.

"Yes, I do won't to go. I might can be of some help."

"When the shootin' starts, you be sure to keep yer head down, it's to pretty to get shot off."

"Yes, I know—you hurry up and go upstairs and wake Pierre. You do have an extra pistol or two in your saddlebags, don't you?"

"Yeah." He pulled on his boots and went out the door.

They were all in the livery stable in record time. When Billy saw La'fay, he started saddling her buckskin for her. Pierre pulled his mount from its stall and started to get his saddle, when Frank stepped in to assist him, and expedite the saddling. He had noticed the navy colt hanging from Pierre's hip, as had everyone. It looked like it was weighing him down.

"When we get to the mine," Frank said, "let's put these hosses in the back stalls and tie the gates."

All was quiet when they walked around to the front door. Forrest was there with Cole, Clell, and two of the miners, with rifles. Wilber and Jim were nervously sitting by the stove drinking coffee. The ladies were in their beds with instructions to stay put and be quiet.

"Captain," Forrest said, "I figure we will leave the two guards on the door, and the rest of us will spread out in hiding places on the west side of the road, so's to not create a cross-fire, and take the fight to them. The back entrance should be okay, cause they can't get to it without going through our fire power. Now, we will probably be out-numbered, but we will have the element of surprise on our side."

"Well Forrest," Frank said, "not only are you a good miner, but you seem to have a militaristic maneuverability skill also. Did Wilber have any idea bout how many robbers there would be?"

"He said best he could figure was bout a dozen. He said they had asked him and his brother to join them, but they refused."

"I have a couple of extra pistols, do you think they might want to help?"

"I done ask'em, Captain, They ain't even never shot a gun. The only'est thing they ever did before coming here to look for gold was dig taters down in the south of Idaho."

"Okay men," Frank said. "let's start gettin' in our positions. They will have to come around to the front on account of that naked ravine running up near the side of us. It's way too deep and steep to cross." They all began to look for good positions along the west side of the road up close to the mine entrance, except La'fay, who stayed just inside the front door with Abner. They all had positioned themselves, with the Captain's instruction, along the opposite side from which the robbers would be approaching. They waited and listened.

About the time they begin to think the robbers weren't coming, a slender sickle of a moon rose in the east through a clear sky, and by that light, they saw them come around the bottom of the ravine in single file and across to the roadway. The moonlight glistening on their guns showed they all carried rifles. Captain Franks men held their fire until the robbers were bunched up about mid-way of them. Frank and his men opened fire. Two of the robbers broke into a fast run making it to the side of the stables and continuing on to the back entrance of the building. La'fay, watching from a slit in the door told Abner, as she started running to the back, that she would stop them. She ran like streaked lightening to the back and saw them enter the building. Drawing and getting off two quick shots, she gut-shot the two before they could get their bearings. Facing Captain Frank, Cole, Billy, Pierre and Forrest, it was not surprising that the other eleven robbers lay dead in the middle of the muddy road.

"Let's drag the two what La'fay got," Billy said, "out front and lay them out with the others. I'll have the undertaker pick them up and bury'em in the graveyard back of town."

Late evening as a blazing sun set in the west, Junior and Susan had left Santa Rosa right after a hardy breakfast and bidding the other Susan a warm goodbye. The railroad track visually arced to the left and headed directly west. After two more days of by-passing two towns, they made camp on the bank of a crystal clear creek flowing gently over the rocks and running under the railroad track. They again had ice-cold baths, and ate some beef jerky before bedding down for the night in the one bedroll that was left. Up at the sign of daylight, they continued their slow wearisome journey. Their talk for some time had been about their dream of someday going back to Missouri and starting them a farm and raising a family. Hanging on to that dream, and their love, unbeknownst to them, was in all reality a way of retaining their sanity.

The following evening they decided to take the spur track and go into the town of Tijeras. It was time again to sleep in a bed. Following the same routine as in Santa Rosa, they had a steak, a bath, and a bed for the night.

After breakfast, and back to the railroad dump, which had now shifted back to a northwest route, they continued their meticulous search for clues of the gold train. Another five days went by with no clues, but a welcomed time to stop in La Jara for the night. It was alike to most western towns of the day, a hotel with restaurant, a livery stable, a blacksmith shop, a mercantile store, a barber shop, and six saloons. Junior and Susan's only interest was in the restaurant/hotel with a bath. For the next five days they bypassed Nagzeezi and Blanco before stopping for the night in Farmington. They had found nothing in the way of clues of the gold train.

Chapter 15

After getting an early start from Farmington, feeling refreshed again, Junior and Susan continued to follow the track north through southern Utah. After cautiously bedding on the ground for another six nights in Navajo and Ute country they stopped in Moab for another hot bath and warm bed. A month elapsed while bypassing most towns like Green River, Wellington, Spanish Fork, Provo, and stopping in Pleasant Grove, Bountiful and Brigham City where they bought new rawhide duds and rain slickers, they continued to Tremonton, treating themselves to steaks, hot baths, and two days in a soft bed. Junior saw to it that their horses were taken good care of and given their fill of oats. A week and a half northwest after leaving Tremonton and staying one night in Shoshone, they passed under the elevated track of the Great Northwest Flyer that runs weekly from Des Moines, Iowa to Boise, Idaho and west to Eugene, Oregon where it connected with trains going north and south. Having never seen anything like an elevated railroad, they stopped and looked it over. Susan dismounted, went under it and looked up. Looking through the many stanchions of framework brought on a sense of vertiginous, causing her to become dazed and weak-kneed.

Her head swimming, she staggered and fell bewildered to the ground. Junior jumped from the mare and kneeling he raised her to a sitting position.

"What happened?" he anxiously asked, "are you alright."

"Yes, I think so, I just got dizzy," said she.

"Here," he said, as he pulled her to her feet. "Walk around a little and see how you feel. We will stop as soon as we find a town."

Susan wasn't long to get on her horse.

"Let's go," she said. "I'm ready to find that town. You don't imagine I could be pregnant, do'ya?"

That statement shot a gigantic new impulse into Junior's daydreaming mind, with many hallucinations of having a son, ending with calling him Franklin Dunlap the third.

"Junior, there's a town up ahead," said Susan.

"What?"—Oh, okay let's stop," said he.

They checked the track switch. It was set for through trains. They took the spur track into Hailey, Idaho for the much needed dinner, bath and bed. As usual they had breakfast before continuing riding track duty. Only about six hours into the day they spotted the enormous building sitting off the west of the track. Junior saw no track switch or any tracks going to the building, He never knew if it was his curiosity or the fact that a storm was brewing, looking like it would start raining at any time that made him decide to stop.

"Susan babe," he said. "Let's go over there and see if we can take shelter from the storm." She reined the buckskin across the neck turning him to cross the track and join Junior. They rode over to the large building. Not seeing anyone around, Junior dismounted and swung open the big door just as the bottom fell out and a deluge of rain started pelting them. He led the mare inside as Susan rode in. She dismounted and stood by him as they had to let their eyesight become accustomed to the dark interior of the building, the first thing Junior spotted was a stack of railroad crossties with rails stretched out beside them. Leading the horses they walked further into the building. There it was sitting right in front of them, a horse car, a Pullman car, boxcar, coal car and locomotive on a partial track.

"We found it Babe," Junior exclaimed triumphantly. "We found the gold train!"

"We'll I be dogged!" said Susan. "I was beginning to think there weren't no such thing. You found it babe, you sure nuff found it. Now what do we do?"

"First thing is to see if the gold is in the boxcar. If it ain't, we try to find out where it is." They searched everything carefully to no avail, until Susan spotted the glint of something under the boxcar door, lodged between a crosstie and the ground. Upon retrieving it she discovered it to be a twenty dollar U.S. gold piece.

The storm had passed and Junior decided to follow the track further north to see where it might go. After riding some twenty miles north, the track turned due west with nothing in sight. "So much for this he said to Susan, "let us go back to where we stayed the night and get bearings to the next settlement of any size."

Back in Hailey, nearing sundown, the people drew them a rough map showing the layout of Fort Hall, Blackfoot and Timberline. They told him there was nothing of any significance to the west until you get all the way to Boise. They drew him the route to Blackfoot over the north of the craters and back down for the most of one day until you come to the wagon road going north for five days to the mining town of Timberline, or south for two days to Blackfoot. "There's been a regular rush on gold mining up there at Timberline." said one of the men. The statement about gold mining struck a nerve with Junior that he couldn't shake off.

"We will need to stay the night and leave in the morning," said Junior.

"You won't your room back with another hot bath?" asked the desk clerk.

"Yeah, that will be fine, we will have supper too," said Junior.

"My wife will wait on'ya in the restaurant. I'll have your bath poured while y'all eat. Y'all enjoy yer supper. If ya'need anything else just holler."

"Thank'ya," said Junior. He and Susan went into the restaurant. They enjoyed the special beef stew with wild herbs like they had never tasted, and yeast bread that had just risen.

Meanwhile at the Timberline hotel, Frank and La'fay were contemplating their reasoning of staying a while longer to be sure the mine would have enough workers to maintain a steady production while they were gone. La'fay suggested that they use Wilber and Jim as adjusters and try to find at least two others to fill in for their own absence. "Maybe Wilber and Jim might know of someone else from around the mountain. I'll ask'em," said she. They didn't know when Pierre may decide to leave and go back to work in Del Rio. "Right now he is working on a stamp head for a $1000 ingot. He said we might have use of some in the future," said she. They would love to have Billy with them, but he would have to be here to oversee the gold shipment. "Esau will be of help providing he's not in Wyoming rounding up horses for the army," said she.

"Yes," Frank said. "I believe we better stay until we are sure everything will run smooth here. You know we will be gone a long time, maybe even forever. I have no doubt that Forrest will do his level best, but before we go, let's make sure he has all the help he needs—of any kind. And I will find out where Pierre's future plans lay."

"Okay," La'fay said, "now get in the bath before the water gets cold, and get to bed with me."

Junior and Susan left Hailey after an early breakfast and headed back north before turning east into the bright sun. They had thought better of mentioning anything about that train. Junior had decided overnight that they would first check out Timberline and if nothing panned out there, they would come back down to Blackfoot. That name rang a bell with Junior. He remembered that the depot agent in Kansas City had told him some years earlier that Blackfoot was where his parents went. Junior and Susan camped the next night high above the craters. Early evening of the next day they intercepted the much traveled wagon road and headed north, supposedly for another five days.

The afternoon of the second day on the wagon-road they stopped next to a large boulder nestled under some majestic pine trees atop a thirty-foot rise by the side of the road. They dismounted and Junior took his water skin from the mare and offered Susan to drink first. As Susan turned her head up and put the spout to her mouth she saw atop the rise, five Indian braves looking down at them from their ponies. She took a drink and before lowering the skin she whispered to Junior about the Indians. Junior looked up and waved a friendly gesture toward them. The Indians being expert horsemen slid their ponies almost perpendicular down the steep slope and came up to them. They were all admiring Susan's yellow hair and making commendatory gestures about it. Junior moved closer to Susan, took his bowie knife from its holster and cut a curl from her hair. He holstered his knife and walked up next to the Indian that seemed to be the leader and handed the curl up to him. The Indians turned and galloped away with the leader holding up his hand with the curl and vociferating as if celebrating a victory.

"I'm damn glad you didn't just give me to'em," said she, in a relieved tone.

"Let's go before they decide to come back after'ya. I noticed a couple of them admiring our hosses too," said Junior.

They mounted up and gave the horses a good run for awhile. Just before nightfall they backed up into the woods, raked up a pile of pine-straw, and rolled out Junior's bedroll on it.

The brisk morning came early and the road quickened its ascension. The higher they climbed the colder it became. The horses were exhaling a visible vapor mist. Junior and Susan stopped and put on their heavy coats. Junior rubbed both of the horse's necks and nose, slapped them gingerly on the chest, and verbally let them know that they were loved.

Beyond the pine trees, the road dipped through a hollow, and Junior and Susan took this better going at the full gallop, letting their horses stretch out to the work. The two had slowed the pace and drew rein at the top of the further slope where they could see the timberline with the bare rock formation reaching into the clouds. They dismounted and marveled at the view. Junior asked Susan if she would like to ride the red mare for a little while. He wished for the horses to get use to both of them, and visa-versa.

As the road once again was ascending it had changed to more bumps than level, more rocks than soil, Junior kept his head high and his eyes fixed on the mountains at which he could see through the double fence of high pine trees. As the road changed, swerved, and twisted snakelike back and forth as mountain trails will do, he had an ever-changing viewpoint and an ever-changing view. But what he saw of them, blue, green, or brown or changing white, was not what filled his soul and kept him smiling: it was his darling sweet Susan, who road on the red mare beside him, leaning toward him, laughing and chatting.

"You see Susan, girl knows you," Junior said. "And she loves you too!"

"As long as you're with me," Susan said. "But if you were away, she'd pitch me into the air and step on me when I hit the ground."

"She'd never buck with you, Susan," said he.

"I can see the side-flare in her eyes," Susan said. "and her ears are trembling, and she keeps a stretch on the reins to make sure that her head belongs to herself."

"Jog her ahead," Junior said, "you'll see that she's as gentle as a lamb, with'ya."

"She'll turn me into a skyrocket," Susan said, "but I don't mind tryin' her." She slapped the shoulder of the red mare, which started instantly off at a long, gliding trot, with head turned to the side as a horse will turn it in order to look back, in this case, to see if Junior was following. But when the mare came to the next bend of the road, rather than round it and pass out of Junior's sight, she suddenly bounded into the air and landed on stiff legs and with arched back. The shock almost slung Susan from the saddle, but with knee and hand she clung to her: and before the red mare leaped again, the shout of Junior checked her like a rope. He trotted the buckskin up to them as Susan straightened herself gasping, she pulled her hat level, and looked at Junior. "She's a real stick of dynamite Junior," she said, "But I told you so!"

Junior shook his head as he dismounted and walked up beside the red mare, he smoothed the silk of her neck with his hand, and spoke to her reproachfully.

"You can't blame her," commented Susan, "She was probably never broken, but only gentled. You can't make a wild hoss fear you, but you can make it love you."

They traded horses, much to the red mares liking, and rounded the bend to see that the road straightened out with an incline straight as an arrow toward the town of Timberline about ten miles further on.

"It don't look like much from here," Junior said, "but it's a ways off. We'll keep the hosses at a slow pace on account of going uphill, but even though, we should make it afore dark sits in."

"I hope we can get somethin' to eat, and a room."

"Yeah, me too. Listen Babe, until we see how things are, it might be best not to mention anything bout me bein' a Marshall. We can use the coin you found to eat and get a room."

"Yeah, okay," said she.

Chapter 16

Nearing sundown, as Junior and Susan rode slowly into Timberline, flabbergasted would be an understatement as to their assessment of the town. Having never been to a mining town, or hell, their innocent consciousness was having trouble excepting the reality of their perception.

If the town had been laid out in blocks, it would have been one block past the livery stable to the Hotel/Restaurant. They tied the horses to a hitching rail in front of the Hotel and went inside to the desk. Mister Parker started to tell them he had no rooms as Junior spoke up.

"Sir, we are Mister and Mrs. Junior Dunbar, we need a room, a bath and some supper." Parker immediately recognized the name and told him he would have to arrange for them a room, "go into the restaurant," he motioned to the door, "supper is being served."

Junior told Susan to go order for them while he took their horses to the livery stable. He went back out the front door as she removed her hat, brushed her hair out and went into the restaurant. La'fay saw the beautiful yellow haired young lady, packing a gun that seemed too big for her size, come into the restaurant, stop and look around for a place to sit. La'fay got up from their big round meeting table, pulled out a chair and motioned for her to come over. La'fay was curious what this young stranger was doing in Timberline.

"Thank'ya Mam," Susan said. "I sure appreciate it. If I could have another chair, my husband will be in when he gets the hosses stabled."

"Sure," La'fay said as she pulled out another chair. "Mine will be down in awhile.—Where y'all from?"

"We're from Missouri, we've been on the trail for quite some time."

"What part of Missouri?" asked La'fay, curiously.

"I'm from Glasgow, and my husband is from Kansas City."

La'fay's curiosity was now at its peak. Maybe, she thought, she's related to someone we know.

"We could very well have been neighbors at one time. What is your name?" La'fay asked.

"My name is Susan, my family name is Spencer. My husband's name is Franklin Dunbar Junior. He's named after his Dad."

La'fay was stunned beyond the realm, or rhythm of her biological clock of ordinary functions. Susan saw her face pale and her eyes glaze over. She wet a cloth napkin in a glass of water and proceeded to wipe the ladies face as Junior came through the door. He rushed over to them and took over the wet napkin detail. Susan sat back down, trembling.

"I don't know what happened Junior, I told her our name and she became white, like I'd hit her or somethin' I don't know what I done."

"It's okay Babe, she's comin' round now. She'll be al'right." Junior said. —"This is my mother." From the looks of Susan, it seemed her time to go off the deep end, but she miraculously survived.

As Captain Frank, Forrest and Pierre entered the room, they stopped momentarily in amazement at La'fay hugging a strange man, before continuing around the table where the Captain joined in the hugging. He looked up at Forrest with moist eyes and said, "he's our son—we thought him dead."

Once the initial welcoming party and a bite of supper had calmed the reunion, Junior and Susan took a hot bath and cleaned up. They spent the remainder of the day and half the night with Frank and La'fay, talking old times and acquainting themselves on the happenings of the past years. Junior told them of his time with the Texas Rangers, but never mentioned anything about being a U.S. Marshal. He told them about being wounded during the skirmish near Fort Osage, and about Edward and Inez Bolton nursing him back to health. They went through the whole story of Junior and Susan's meeting and eventual wedding. La'fay told them about winning the gold mine in a poker game and coming to Timberline. Once the homecoming reunion had about played out, and everyone was lovingly happy, Junior and Susan went to their room, with unknown facts being kept secret from both parties. Come morning, Junior and Susan would go to see the mine with Frank and La'fay.

After a hot breakfast with the people of the mine, Junior and Susan saw more of the repugnant mining town on the way to the mine with Frank, La'fay, and their people. La'fay took Susan under her wing and showed her all of the operations of the mine, while Junior's Dad did the same with him. He also told him of his plans to try to use his gold for an enticement to sway the Government to let up on the Southern people and reinstate the Southern politicians to State offices, so the farmers could start working their farms and marketing their produce to the benefit of helping eliminate the depression. Frank laid out his whole plan without mentioning anything about the stolen gold.

Junior, without letting his Dad know, was very skeptical about the mine producing enough gold to finance such a meaningful brain-storm. He sensed and shared his Dad's passion about the rebirth of the South, and he greatly liked the idea. He and Susan had dreamed of someday having them a farm so they could raise their kids as they were raised. He also liked the mine. He just couldn't see it putting out the amount of gold needed for such an undertaking. His skepticism, much to his consternation, made him wonder if these people were re-minting gold from the train. The train was as far as it could get to this mine. *"No, my Mother would never go along with such a scheme!—but then—I think I might snoop around some."*

"Hey Junior," Cole Younger said, "you probably don't remember me, I'm Cole Younger. I remember seeing you at Lawrence, Kansas. You were with Bill Anderson. I had my own personal problems of seeing you and Jesse and many other young men at a massacre like that one. I'm glad to see you're okay. I heard you been separated from yer Ma and Pa fer some few years now. It's good ta'see you back with'em."

"Hi Mister Younger—Yeah, I remember you." The first thing Captain Frank did early that morning was to let everyone know not to mention the Union gold or the train. "It's no use letting anyone know anything that is not absolutely necessary. I'll tell Junior about it when the proper time comes to do so."

The more the Union gold weighed on Junior's mind, the more suspicious he became. He knew from common sense that the gold train didn't just happen to come this close to Timberline without a reason. What reason could there be except to fulfill the desires of a scheming self proclaimed redeemer. The sensible thing for him to do would be to re-mint it for private use in order to sufficiently carry out his plan. Like his Dad had said to him, We will always be stepped on and held down unless someone takes the initiative and does something about it. *"I guess Dad was right, but he's fighting the government—Hell, so what, I fought them when I was a bushwhacker, the same as he fought the Union when he was in the Army. I can't say my Dad is wrong—if he is, then my Mother is too—and I have been and didn't think I was—Hell, I still don't think I was. Can Dad pull this off? Can Susan and I someday have a farm to raise our kids on?"*

Frank, La'fay, Junior and Susan were the only ones left in the restaurant. All the others had gone to the mine.

"Well Dad," Junior asked. "When do you plan to leave for Missouri?"

Frank took a sip of coffee before speaking. "Your Mother and I have to see what we can do about some more people to work the minting procedures with Forrest and Pierre before we leave. As soon as we are satisfied that it will continue to operate sufficiently, then we will leave."

"Are the jobs in mind easy to learn, or do they take highly skilled people?" asked Junior.

"No, nothing is real hard to learn." La'fay said. "Most anyone can pick it up in a couple of hours. How all the procedures fit together is important, but Forrest takes care of that—Frank we could sure use about four more adjusters.

They could go on the front end of the table, ya'know, toward the door, We could divide the scales between each two."

"That would certainly speed up production," said Frank, "trouble is, where we go'na find'em."

"Advertize," said Junior, "spread the word around town that the mine is hiring. Put up some signs."

They all looked dumbfoundedly at Junior. "Well hell," he said, "it may work, it's surely worth a try."

"I'll have one of the girls make some signs," said La'fay.

"Oh, by the way Dad," Junior asked. "How did y'all manage to get all of Grant's gold up here from the train in the old open pit mining building."

There was deadly silence!!! The only thing heard for a full two minutes were a couple of flies mating on the window glass.

Finally Frank spoke," La'fay, you and Susan go on to the mine and get the signs started. Go upstairs first and put on your guns," he looked at Junior, "can she shoot?"

"Yeah, better than anybody I know," Junior said, "I wouldn't want to go up again'er."

"No Frank," La'fay said, "I want to hear this. We'll go later." Susan had gotten up to go, but sit back down.

"Before you start any explaining," Junior said, "there is one humungous mistake you have made. Do you realize when the Army finds that train—and they will, just like I did. They will know the gold came to Timberline, because it's the only logical place for it to be taken and melted down. It's like parking the train in your front yard. Then when you go to Grant's people they will know that you were the culprit who stole their gold. And I'm afraid they will frown quite heavily on giving you any kind of considerateness or compensation for the return of their gold."

Franks face paled, he tried to say something but the words would not come. His lips issued a slight murmur as he stared unknowingly at Junior.

"I looked the situation over very carefully and saw right away what I would have done, had it been me. Do you wish to hear the only salvation for your scheme?"

Frank nodded his head as he continued to stare at Junior.

"We have to get rid of the train," uttered Junior.

Frank spoke more clearly. "How Junior, how do you get rid of a big train?—I can see where you're right about them finding it right in my front yard, like ya'said, but how in God's name do'ya just get rid of a train?"

"We will need as many able bodied men as you can possibly get. I saw shovels and sledge hammers, and box's of spikes beside where the train is. We will need all the rails and crossties we can salvage. We have to put the switching apparatus back out front and lay the track to connect with it. We'll fire up the boiler and build a head of steam, then back it out and go onto the track. When we pull ahead, we will take the switching unit out and put it on the train to be used later, then when we get to where the wagon trail goes east and over the craters, we will install the switching apparatus and lay track to take us the same way the road goes. If you remember noticing it, there is a steep incline from the top to the first crater far below. We lay the track high above the crater and slant it down at the right angle straight toward the edge of the crater. From there, nothing could hold that heavy train back once it started down the slope. It would sink two or three hundred feet into the green watery depths of oblivion. This is go'na take a lot of hard work— but then, no more train. If we don't have enough rails and crossties, we can keep taking them up behind us and laying them in front. We will have to take them all up and camouflage the area anyway, to conceal the presence of there ever having been a train or track there. And, don't let us forget, we will take the crossties back to the building and do away with them in the tailing pits out in back of the building. I don't know if they would float or not, but let's not take that chance. We will need a wagon with a four up team of mules."

"Let's go to the mine and let Forrest and Billy know of my stupidity, and what we must do to make things right," said a lowly downcast Franklin.

"Dad, don't be whippin' yerself over one missed detail. You have undoubtedly had hundreds of them that you did get right. So buck up and conduct yerself like the leader that ya'are. Don't let yer people see you lookin' down in the dumps."

Frank cracked a smile and said. "Ya'know, you're treating me like I used to treat you when you made mistakes."

"I don't know where you're comin' from Dad, I never made mistakes," said Junior as they all broke out in laughter.

"Just one thing, Junior," Frank asked, "why were you even in that old mine building?"

"I was lookin' for Grant's gold.—I was commissioned by the President to find his gold." He took his badge from his pocket and pitched it on the table. "If I could find it, so will others."

La'fay picked up the badge, looked at it and handed it to Frank. Frank handed it back to Junior, and he returned it to his vest pocket.

"We best do as Junior say's," La'fay said, "and get rid of the train."

They all looked unknowingly at Junior.

"Well hell," Junior said, "Did you expect me to turn'ya in, and see my parents hanged. Susan, you and mama get yer guns and go on to the mine, we'll be along after awhile."

Chapter 17

Frank told Junior it was best to take his and Susan's horse to the stable at the mine. They went to the stable, saddled the horses, and secured the one bedroll and bearskin coats on with saddle ties. Junior took the red mare and Frank the buckskin gelding, they led them outside, mounted and walked them slowly to the mine.

"Isn't that the little spitfire mustang you led around all over the place before I left to join the army?" asked Frank.

"Yep, this is her, "Junior said, "I got her back."

"So you did finally break her?"

"No, I only gentled her. Like Susan said. You can't make a wild horse fear you, but you can make it love you—or something like that. I didn't understand it, but no, I didn't break her, and yes, she does love me—she has certainly shown me that oodles of times. Like the time she dragged me to the Bolton farm when I was shot. I told'ya bout that."

"Well she certainly has matured and has fine lines," said Frank.

"Yeah, well she's grown up. She was just a little kid girl back then."

"Stay to the left," said Frank, "and go up to the far stalls by the other hosses."

Inside the mine and minting building, Frank had his people to gather around, and he told them the drastic oversight that Junior had pointed out, and the reasoning as to why it had to be rectified. He blamed himself but did not dwell on the subject of fault. He told Forrest to work on getting all available hands that he could. "Take anybody that can handle a shovel or drive a spike," said he.

Forrest told him that La'fay had clued him in on what had to be done. Excluding her and Susan, and Pierre and the ladies, he could only think of eleven men. "That would be myself, you and Junior, Billy, Cole and Clell, Wilber and Jim, and the three men in the mine."

"Where is La'fay and Susan?" asked Frank.

"They're in the back with some of the ladies making up signs to put around town for hiring people to work in the mine."

"If the signs get good response," Junior said, "let's try to find some men for the railroad work. Maybe there will be a few that has had railroad experience. At any rate, if we find any, they will have to seem trustworthy and swear secrecy on whatever idol they believe in, to not every mention, even if asked, of every having worked on the job. If you find any such men, pay them well above what they would make in the mine."

La'fay and Susan came up front with six signs, holding up one for all to see. "We would like for Cole, Clell and Billy to accompany us in putting up the signs around town."

"Do you have a hammer and some small nails," asked Cole.

"Yes" said she.

"It's too late to do it today," said Billy, "let's meet at the restaurant in the morning, and do it first thing."

It took little time to put the signs up in strategic places throughout town. Before they got to the mine some men were following them. Once inside La'fay told Forrest to get ready to start hiring. Before Forrest could sufficiently assess his thoughts he had about twenty people asking for him with more on the way. Seeing the most grateful situation, Billy stepped up to help him. He held his hands to get the men's attention.

"Men, if y'all will all stand over this way," he motioned to the side of the room, "I will let you know of the procedures. Mister Abernathy will see each of you independently. But first I will tell you that there are two job categories, and separate you in groups depending on which you wish to apply for. First is working in the minting facilities of the mine. The second job will be laying a short railroad track. If any of you have experience on railroad construction, let me see a show of hands." About eight men raised their hands. "Alright, I want to separate y'all. The railroad men stand over to this side," said he, as he motioned to the side. "Now, the construction job will pay considerable more than the mine job. But will not last as long. If there be other able bodied men who might like this work, step over with the others." About a dozen more men moved over with the railroad men. "I see Mister Abernathy has a table sit up to start interviewing. He is going to take the railroad men first. So the rest of you just take is easy until he can get to you. Mister Goodman has made fresh coffee at the stove, y'all can help yerself."

"I see we have about 20 men here," said Forrest, "that's good. Now men the first thing I want each of you to do is sign this oath stating that you will never under any circumstance, including duress, talk about the railroad what we're going to construct, or the train that will be moved on it. This will mean no talk even among yerselves. Now, I estimate this work will take, at the most, maybe two weeks. Now since this will be the extent of your employment, we will pay each of you $200 in Timberline gold." He glanced at Captain Frank for approval, and got a thumbs-up. "Come up to the table one at a time to sign the oath and give me yer name. We will furnish each of you with a bed roll and rain slicker. Now, as y'all can see, I'm figuring what to do, as I go along.—As we will be takin' a mule team and wagon fer use on the job, I'll see to it that we take fixings and utensils for cookin, and designate somebody fer the cook. Okay men, up here one at a time."

"I see that Madame La'fay," Billy said, "has corralled about a dozen men, including two ladies back at the minting table. She is showing them what the coining work consist of."

"That's good Billy," said Captain Frank, "You can dismiss any leftovers."

By early evening the next day, all was set to go start moving the train. Frank and Junior, with Billy, would oversee the railroad work. Forrest would continue as normal at the mine. The mine hands would continue to keep the gold coming. Susan would stay and work with La'fay. Pierre would continue engraving the thousand dollar ingot. La'fay would lengthen the adjuster table toward the front door. All was happy that the mine didn't have to shut down to move the train.

Frank had decided to take two mule teams. Most of the men would be able to ride instead of having to walk, although some would rather walk as long as they didn't have to lug their possessions.

Once they reached the big open-pit mine and minting barn, Frank told them what had to be done. The experienced track men got busy, while showing others how to help. They first went down the track a ways and took up a section of matching rails that they replaced with switching rails from the building. They left the straight tracks which they removed to have to put back later. Other men with shovels rebuilt the dump while others started laying track into the barn. Frank noticed how the work progressed with ease. The second day they backed the train up, switching it onto the track and switched the track back to go forward. They had loaded crossties, rails and spikes into the boxcar and horse-car. When the train pulled forward past the switching tracks, they were taken up and put on the train.

Everything went well with installing the switching tracks for connection onto newly laid track heading toward the northern rim of the glaciers. Once they started the journey to the top of the glacier, they took Junior's advice on running about ten tracks and moving crossties and rails from the back to the front as they proceeded forward. Once they reached the top they slanted the angle down so as to go over the edge about midway of the crater rim. When they were all set the engineer started the train down and jumped from it. They all backed up and watched. A sight to behold for a lifetime, the entire train was mid-air fifty feet above the water. It all crashed into the water jumbling together and crying like a million scalded cats. The train bunched together with at least three feet of each car sticking out of the water. It set there creaking, groaning and mourning lamentably like it was alive for a good ten minutes while everyone experienced an unnerving cold sweat, in fear that it wasn't going down. And then with one last groaning scream it gave way and went down pulling a giant swirl of boiling green water down behind it, just as Junior had envisioned it, except for the unanticipated scare. On the fifth day of moving the train, they now only had to take the track and crossties up on their way back. They also took out the switching tracks and replaced them with straight tracks. The small dump was shoveled down level, and the other track going into the barn was removed. Everything was leveled out and the ground camouflaged to hide any traces of there ever being a train track there. All the left over crossties, rails and spikes were buried far out in the tailing pits. Junior didn't have much to do, so he had helped one of the men with the cooking. In eight days the job was finished. Frank got a couple of the men to help take down and load another melting pot and six more sets of scales that they found in a back store room. Frank had brought a sack of fifty dollar gold pieces with him and paid the men. He thought that perhaps they might not want to make the trip back to Timberline. He was right, only two of the new men went back with him, Junior, and Billy. They were in hopes of getting jobs in the mine.

Frank found that the minting was well in hand and complemented La'fay and Forrest. He asked Forrest to find a place to use the two men that had returned with him and Junior. "I'll have them to work in the mine helping move out the tailings so the experienced miners don't have to stop to do it." Cole took control of the mule teams and took the loaded wagon to the front entrance. With help everything was unloaded through the front door. Forrest immediately showed Clell and a couple other men where to set up the melting pot. "Exactly like the others," said he. He also showed Frank that La'fay had gotten Cole, Clell and some others to build an eight foot adjuster bench extension toward the front. She also had bought six more stools, and had twelve adjusters now working, including Wilber and Jim. She was overjoyed to see the six new scales.

Alice and a couple of the other ladies were teaching and overseeing the new adjusters. La'fay took Frank by the arm.

"Come on, let's go to the hotel and clean you up." Frank looked around. "If you're lookin' for Junior," La'fay said, "he and Susan left as soon as y'all arrived."

"No, I was lookin'fer Billy," said he.

"He went off to do some of his regular Sheriff'n work," said she.

As they walked in the door they heard Mister Parker yell into the back. "We need another tub of hot water poured in number 10."

Chapter 18

The panic of 1873 was a world-wide depression that started when the stock market crashed in Vienna in June 1873. Unsettled markets soon spread to Berlin, and throughout Europe. Three months later, the Panic spread to the United States when three major banks stopped making payments. The New York Warehouse & Security Company on September 8, Kenyon, Cox, & Company on September 13, and the largest bank, Jay Cooke & Company, on September 18. On September 20, the New York Stock Exchange shut down for ten days. All of these events created a depression that lasted five years in the United States, ruined thousands of businesses, depressed daily wages by 25% from 1873 to 1876, and brought the unemployment rate up to 14%. Some 89 out of 364 American railroads went bankrupt.

The recompense of the Panic in the United States included over-expansion in the railroad industry after the Civil War, losses in the Chicago and Boston fires of 1871 and 1872, respectively, and insatiable speculation by Wall Street financiers. All of this growth was done on borrowed money by many banks in the United States having over-speculated in the railroad industry, and huge loans to the government for a four billion dollar gold purchase.

After breakfast the following morning, Frank was laying out plans. "As y'all all know La'fay and I, along with Junior and Susan, will be leaving today. We'll get settled in Kansas City, Missouri, where with Junior's help I will start preliminary work on the finality of our League's pursuit. We will have help from known and trusted friends in the area, so hopefully it won't take long to instigate a meeting with the President. Now, as far as the situation here goes, you all know that Forrest Abernathy is the boss over the mine and all mining decisions. As a matter of fact, I haven't had a chance to tell him yet, but for about two weeks now, he has been part owner of the Timberline mine." Forrest hung his head down in his hands. Everyone applauded.

"Billy," said Frank. "I want you to put someone in Blackfoot on a permanent basis to check with the telegraph office daily for messages. I will also let you know where to wire me in emergency. When we are ready to ship, your man will have to come here to let you know. I realize it will take over two weeks for it to get under way. I'll give you all the information by wire as to where it will go. Cole and Clell will accompany you along with some Union soldiers. I will take care of having Army Intelligence to contact Fort Hall Army headquarters. Tell Clell to get Alice passage and take her with him when they accompany the gold shipment. Give all at the mine our best and tell them, hopefully we will someday come and visit. And as there is a great possibility that there could be soldiers sent up here to check out the mine, still looking for Grant's gold, you need to hide the stash that you're working from. I would suggest you put in a door on the other side in the back going out behind the mule corral and a gate into the back of the corral. Then dig a hole inside the corral to put the sacks in. You can cover it all with about a foot of dirt and keep hay scattered over it. Only take out enough to fill the melting pots as needed, only when it's safe to do so. Hopefully they won't come up here but it's best to be safe." A devious smile crept across Frank's face as he continued. "You know they will be scouring the countryside south of here looking for the gold train."

"I think that we should plant rumors of the train being down in Mexico," Junior said, "It could have been sidetracked along in New Mexico somewhere and waited for the east bound train to pass before continuing on to Tucson and turning south through Nogales into Mexico."

Pierre spoke up, "Junior, you might want to change your story," he said," There is a railroad track running from the back of the Del Rio mining and minting facility to the New Orleans mint. At one time Mexico used to ship some of their gold to New Orleans to be stamped for Mexican coins. Then those coins were shipped from there to Mexico City, for redistribution into the economy, on the same track directly back by Del Rio, and intercepting a track running from the mine due south to Mexico City. I'll lay it all out in detail for you before you leave."

La'fay interjected. "In case of emergency before any of this transpires we will be staying at the Grand Hotel in South Kansas City."

After eight days and nights of sleeping in bedrolls on raked up pine-straw, and still wearing their buckskin clothes and side-arms, with their mounts safely in horse-cars, they boarded the Great Northern Flyer in Blackfoot, to Des Moines, with transfer on the Union Pacific to Kansas City.

Frank carried with him, three ingot bars and a sack full of fifty dollar Timberline gold pieces. He took the bars in a leather carrying case, and La'fay took the coins in a similar case. They kept the bags in hand on the train, the transfer, and the Union Pacific to Kansas City, with a well armed young couple keeping a close watch on them.

Before going to the bank, they had to assure themselves that they would still have an address at the Grand Hotel of South Kansas City. When the train wranglers brought their horses down the ramp to them, they tightened the saddle cinches, mounted and hung their leather cases on the saddle pommels. Junior and Susan babied their mounts with rubs and pats. Then the four of them rode through Kansas City to the Grand Hotel.

The hotel manager and owner did not immediately recognize them. He paled slightly to see them looking like western cattle drovers in their leathers and wearing side-arms. He whispered their names as if a question.

La'fay told him it was truly them and explained it away by saying that they had been hunting in the wilds of Idaho.

The manager told them they could have their same home on the third floor. He said nobody else in town, the way things are, can afford it. He paused, looking at them again, and asked if they wanted it. He said he would reduce their lease. La'fay told him yes, and don't worry about the lease, just draw it up and they will pay him the same as it was. The owner was overjoyed to have them back. "The four trunks you packed are still in the attic, I'll have them brought down for you," said he.

La'fay asked him also for his best room for Junior and Susan, as she introduced them. Frank suggested they have a bath and change clothes before doing anything else. "We have four horses tied to the rail. Do you have a man that can take them to the livery?" The owner called one of his men. "We'll go out with him to get our saddlebags," said Frank. While Frank and Junior were out, La'fay paid the owner six hundred dollars in fifty dollar gold pieces for the first years lease, and three hundred for Junior and Susan's room, also for a year. He put the remainder of his bellmen staff to work getting their luggage from the attic and pouring a bath in their third floor home, and another in Junior and Susan's room, also on the third floor. Frank and Junior came in with the saddle-bags, Frank retrieved his leather carrying case, and got on the elevator with La'fay, Junior and Susan.

La'fay finished bathing and slipped into one of her old casual dresses. She had also given one to Susan. "Me and Susan are going out to the beauty parlor," she said, as Frank was getting into the bath. "The restaurant will be open for supper in two hours, We'll be back by then, and we will all have us a good meal. I'll set our cases in the closet and lock it."

"Okay, Babe-doll, that'll be fine," said he.

The next morning after breakfast, and half a night of telling La'fay how extraordinarily beautiful she was. Frank went to the bank and deposited two gold bars. He then rented a two-up fringed carriage for four, with two beautiful solid white carriage geldings, and he, La'fay, Junior, and Susan headed out, with the men in their best old duds, toward Blue Springs lake and to the home of Esau and Maria Jones. Frank noticed that La'fay and Susan had on gorgeous new dresses and hats. They had gone to the ladies boutique after the beauty parlor.

They stopped to view the beautiful lake for a while before continuing on to the Jones Horse Farm. Once through the front gate, as before, Frank cantered the team around the house to the back. As he stopped, Jim Conners came from the barn and took hold of the team.

"Madame La'fay and Mister Frank," Jim said, smiling and showing age, "how have you folks been."

As La'fay attempted to answer him, out the back door ran Christian and Christine. As they hugged her, she was astounded as to how much they had grown. But then she realized it had been 4 years since she had seen them. La'fay was introducing the exceptionally great looking kids to Junior and Susan when Maria ran out shrieking and grabbed La'fay, dancing around with her. "Are you back to stay," she asked excitedly.

"I certainly hope so," said La'fay as they continued to hug.

Next out of the house came Esau, followed by Frank and Jesse James. Everyone had gotten out of the carriage and Jim was taking it to the barn.

When Esau, Frank and Jesse noticed that the younger man was Junior Dunlap, a reunion celebration erupted to beat all surprise reunions. They all whooped and hollered and jounced around like little kids. Frank James finally paid his respects to the old folks, hugging Frank Dunbar and expressing compliments to La'fay. Junior introduced Susan as his redeeming angel.

"Mine's in the house," said Jesse, "with little Jesse. Frank's wife is inside too."

"Let us all go inside," Esau said. "where we can be comfortable and talk. Maria, tell Birdie how many will be for dinner. That should make her day."

"Let's not put her to any trouble," said La'fay.

"She won't mind, La'fay." Maria said, "she loves to cook—you know that, come on in."

Inside the drawing room, Jesse found Zee and little Jesse Edward (About two years of age) sitting on the floor playing. Zee jumped up to see other people coming in.

"Folks, this is my beloved wife Zee, and little Jesse Edward," said Jesse. Susan picked up little Jesse, hugged and kissed him, and hugged Zee.

"I'm Susan,—Junior's wife," said she.

Once salutations were made all around, down the stairs came Frank's wife, Annie, an exquisitely beautiful young lady and a person of impeccable respectability. The salutations began again.

Annie's father, the well-to-do Samuel Ralston, who had served in the Confederate Army under Missouri's adored General Shelby, even though knowing Frank James was fond of Shakespeare and had a speaking knowledge of German and Spanish, did not approve of his courtship with Annie. She, however was very much in love with Frank, and having a mind of her own, married him near Independence, Missouri in 1875. She was twenty-two and Frank was thirty years old. They would later have one child, a son christened Robert Frank James. The happiest period of their lives was their residence for several years near Nashville, Tennessee, where under the name of Woodson, the rather studious and thoughtful Frank farmed and engaged in other rural occupations unrelated to robbery.

After visiting with Esau for about a week, Mister and Mrs. Jackson (Jesse and Zee), by buggy took Jesse Edward to Kearney, to visit awhile with his grandmother Zerelda James Samuels, also Zee's aunt after which she was named.

Afterward Mister and Mrs. Woodson (Frank and Annie), and Mister and Mrs. Jackson boarded an express train for New York City. Jesse, Frank and their wives remained in New York under fictitious names for two months. Frank and Annie took in virtually every play on Broadway. Jesse and Zee relaxed at the Saratoga Springs spa. They all, living a grandeur lifestyle, enjoyed themselves immensely. It was in New York, that Annie told Frank he was going to be a father.

During their stay with Esau and Maria, Esau, Junior and the James brothers renewed their friendship. They brought up old forgotten situations, like the time Esua ran into Frank and Jesse in California at their Uncle's hot sulfur springs spa in San Luis Obispo. Esau at that time was a bounty hunter, and was looking for Maria at the Mission San Miguel Archangel in San Miguel. Not to collect bounty on her, but to rescue her from a convent where she was becoming a nun. He was madly in love with her. He stopped at the spa and there was Frank and Jesse in retreat at their Uncle's spa, which was a favorite place for them to disappear from time to time. Jesse playfully accused Esau of hunting them down to collect the reward on their heads. He stayed with them a couple of days and indulged in a few sulfur baths, an experience he never forgot.

Frank told Susan that he remembered her well, although she was a little barefoot kid. He couldn't mistake those big blue eyes. He and Jesse had stopped by the Spencer place to see her brother Orville on business and there she was outside with Orville teaching her gunmanship. He couldn't help but notice that the Navy Colt looked nearly as big as her.

Jesse asked Junior about the killing of his good friend, Archie Clements. He had always blamed Bacon Montgomery with his death. Junior told him the whole story of how it happened and of himself being wounded and nursed back to health by the Bolton family. But yes, Bacon Montgomery, although he did not do the actual shooting, was certainly responsible.

Chapter 19

Esau Jones had many private discussions with Franklin and Junior Dunbar, about the best way to go about having a meeting with President Grant. They worked on how to handle the meeting once it was accomplished. They knew it would be like dodging arrows to get the point across that it would be good for the economy and help to alleviate the depression.

"I have been secretly doing a bit of investigating," Esau said, "There has recently been appointed a new Secretary of Treasury by the name of Benjamin Bristow. I happened to know, through the sale of a team of buggy hosses, a man that knows Bristow. I had him to ask Bristow how I might get an audience with President Grant. I told him I wished to talk to him personally about selling him some fine hosses. He does keep some hosses and has a love of raising them. Anyway, awhile later the man came to see me to let me know that anyone seeing the President must first go through his private secretary, Mister Orville E. Babcock. This Babcock has just recently been acquitted with the help of the President on charges of being implicated in the Whiskey Ring Graft trials. Anyway it seems he's the one to go through to see the President."

"Did you ever go to Wyoming with the soldiers to get some hosses for the Army?" asked Frank.

"Oh yes," said Esau, "bout three years ago. What a fiasco that was. We did bring some hosses back, but I laughed my tail off the whole trip watching those soldiers trying to be cowboys. I've been holding my breath hoping they don't want any more hosses."

"What do you think may be the next step in getting Dad in to see Grant," asked Junior.

"We've got to instigate a way to see Babcock and incite him with a teaser," said Esau, "you know, like hanging a carrot out in front of a donkey to make him pull the wagon."

"You have any ideas?" asked Junior.

"Since we know that he is a crook from skimming profits in the Whiskey Ring affair," Esau said, "I believe if he could see a chance of pocketing some of the gold, it might just be our ticket. I'll work on a way, Frank, for you to meet with Babcock. It may take some clever conniving on your part to put this over. I think you should play the part of the naive, yet merciful patriotic donor of multi-millions and let him be the one, if he asks, to show a sample of the gold to the President. But you should stand firm on an audience with the President, after they've had time to have their mineralogist approve the area of the gold's disposition, like you explained the difference in color to me."

"My miner, Forrest Albernaty, one of the best and most honest people there is, made up the gold that we brought with us from pure northwestern gold without any of the Del Rio gold mixed in it. So there will be no doubt of the area from where it was mined and struck."

"I'll get right on to getting you in to see Babcock," Esau said, "I do believe this to be the best way to go. Take the bull by the horns, so to speak."

"Yeah," Frank said, "Or the President by the shorthairs."

Junior laughed, "Let's go to the dining room, I believe they have put supper on."

Maria, La'fay, and Susan were having their own little meeting at the dinner table, telling bedtime secrets about their men.

"Why didn't you call," said Esau.

"We didn't want to disturb your meeting," said Maria, as Susan giggled.

"What's funny?" asked Junior.

"Nothing," Susan said. "It's an inside joke." All the ladies laughed. The men looked at one another curiously.

"What's to eat," asked Esau, as they sat down at the table.

Christian and Christine came down the stairs. Christine asked, "Why did you not call us for supper." Her mother said they were having too much fun and they all laughed again. Esau looked at his daughter and shrugged.

Three weeks later, the four Dunbar's, after living a short life of leisure, sat in the Grand Hotel restaurant having breakfast when Esau Jones walked in and joined them. After greetings all around, Esau's expression changed to that of strictly business.

"Captain Frank" he said. "The acquaintance I spoke of talked to Benjamin Bristow, and he has made an appointment for you with the President's private secretary, Orville Babcock, for whenever you can get there."

Captain Frank stared expressionless at Esau for a long moment before speaking. "What did your man say to Bristow?"

"He told him you were independently wealthy and wished to show him how to end the depression."

Two days hence, the Dunbar men, groomed and donning new suits and boots, along with their wives, boarded the Union Pacific express train from Kansas City to Washington, D.C. They acquired joining rooms only a short way from the White House, and the Capital, at the National Hotel. Junior and Frank waited patiently in Frank and La'fays room for the ladies to freshen up before going down to the restaurant for supper.

"Dad, I think that I should make my appearance the first thing in the morning, concerning our discussion about the train."

"Yes, it may be best so it will hinder his first thoughts about the possibility of me re-minting his gold."

They had discussed this plan before leaving the Timberline hotel. Junior would introduce himself as the presidential Marshal that had been commissioned to locate the gold train, and give them his fabricated story about the train being somewhere in central Mexico. He had the story all laid out in his mind as to how it was undoubtedly masterminded by Benito Juarez who was by this time back in his Mexico City palace.

"I will take one fifty dollar gold piece with me," Junior said, "and if the opportunity arises, I will lay the groundwork for your meeting."

"In what way?" asked Frank.

"In my search, I heard of a fabulously wealthy gold mine and minting facility in Timberline, and my curiosity had me to check it out. My first thoughts were that the gold could be re-minted. But then on meeting and talking to the owner, and looking over the mine and minting process and seeing literally a multitude of ten thousand dollar gold bars, with no indication of dishonest or blameworthy activities. All feelings of dishonesty quickly left me when he showed me inside the mine and explained to me how they had run into an alluvium deposit of an ancient riverbed and were working it right on its bedrock. I saw nuggets in their sluice box as big as hen eggs."

Frank, La'fay and Susan were listening intently to Junior. He took a drink of water and continued. "I will say to him that the mine owner took me into his confidence and told me he was going to try to see President Grant and offer to help him as best he could to alleviate the terrible distress of the dreadful depression. He said he, as of now, had a million dollars and could have the same amount every six months. I will tell the man, know only as Captain Frank, said he could show him the way to save the Union and possible his presidency for another term. Then I will tell him that Captain Frank is here in Washington. I met him yesterday and know where he is staying. If you like I will send him to see you, I know that is what he wants, he just doesn't know how to go about getting an audience with you."

"That all sounds good son," Captain Frank said, "I sure hope you can pull it off. It would eliminate the go betweens. When are you going?"

"It's mid-mornin', I might as well go now, while I've got my spill all worked out. So it's off to the capital building— wish me luck."

La'fay hugged him, Susan kissed him and said. "You can do it darlin', I have faith in you."

It was only a short walk from the Hotel to the Capital. As Junior turned onto the walkway heading toward the capital, two capital guards stopped him for identification. He showed them his badge, told them his name was Junior Barstow, and that he had to report to either Lester Musgrove, or Henry Arbuckle. They acknowledged his identification and told him to see the man at the desk just inside the door. He told the man at the desk the same thing over again. The deskman made two calls and told Junior that neither man was available.

"Sir," Junior said somewhat aggravated, "I am a presidential Marshal with a most important message for the president. If I am not sent in to see him, I'm sure he is going to be most displeased by me getting a run-around from the hired help. Now you get someone out here to take me to see the president, immediately."

The deskman made another call and said, "Sir, you need to come to the lobby, and help me resolve a slight dilemma—thank you sir." In a matter of minutes the president's personal secretary, Orville E. Babcock came to the desk. He looked at Junior's badge and told him politely to come with him to his office. In Babcock's office he was offered a chair and Babcock asked what this meeting was about.

"Sir," he said. "Back in the latter part of October 1874 after the depression hit us, I was indirectly commissioned by the president to search for the stolen gold train. It has been a long and tedious search. Now, I'll tell you off the top, I have not seen the train but I do know where it is. The story I have for you is of the utmost importance. I know the president will want to hear this first hand, so I would like an audience with him—and certainly it may include you too." Babcock started an adversative statement and Junior stopped him. "Mister Babcock, I'll not mince my words. This is of the utmost importance to the outcome of our nation, and when the president finds out I was stopped from seeing him, I can assure you there will be hell to pay."

Babcock motioned for a guard to come over and told him to search Mister Barstow, and then tell the President that I will be bringing someone in to see him.

Upstairs in the President's office Junior was offered a seat in a plush chair in front of the President's desk. Babcock made the introductions and told the president it was about the missing gold train. Grant's face lit up. "Did you find it?"

"No Sir," Junior said, but I know without a doubt where it is." Junior went through his story as he had rehearsed it numerous times. The train is somewhere in the outskirts of Mexico City where they are re-minting your gold and making it into Mexican money."

"Do you have any proof of that?"

"Mister President, Sir leave me finish my story and you will see my reasoning."

"First let me tell you of a railroad going from the back of the Del Rio facility east to New Orleans. It runs from Del Rio south through Laredo to Brownsville and back up the coast through Corpus Christi, through Houston, Lake Charles and Morgan City into the New Orleans Mint. Now that is not where they took the gold. I wanted to point out this route because it was used extensively to take Mexican gold to the mint for minting Mexican coins, before the mint was closed after the war started. Now, where did your gold train go?—It took a route leaving Laredo directly into the heartland of Mexico, through Monterrey, San Luis Potosi, and to Ciudad de Mexico, Mexico City. There are three minting facilities around Mexico City. Not to sound pert Sir, But you can bet your bottom dollar that Generalissimo Benito Juarez is drinkin' red wine in his glorious palace and laughing about re-minting your gold into Mexican coins."

Junior took a handkerchief from his pocket and wiped his brow before continuing. "Now Sir, I would dare venture down into Mexico to look for the train, as it would be sheer suicide. And one more thing I will point out if you're considering taking troops down there. Although I'm sure you realize this, being the war strategist that you are, for which I would like to take this time to commend you. Anyway I wanted to say this, Benito Juarez's Federallies out number your troops somewhere in the ratio of eight to 1. Not like the revolutionist we fought on the border when I was a Texas Ranger. Also our nation could not afford a war, what with the depression.—There is one more thing I wish to bring up." He told him about the Timberline mine exactly as he had related his speech to Captain Frank.

"If I am not further needed Sir," he said politely, "I'll turn in my badge and wish the best for our Union."

"You hold on to the badge Mister Barstow." Grant said, and have Captain Frank in my office tomorrow around ten a.m."

"Yes Sir, Mister President."

Chapter 20

The breakfast alarm came early for the Dunbar's. Frank and Junior rushed to get shaven and cleaned up before going down to eat breakfast. The ladies were ready by the time they were.

Captain Frank's nerves were on edge as they tried to eat breakfast. Junior comforted him, telling him that Grant is probably more afraid than him. "Just look at him as being below you, and tell him how the moon rises. Tell him what he has to do to get your money, no if's, ands or buts. Hell Dad, you could always sell your gold to Britton or Spain if he doesn't want to go along with you on your considerations, Just buckle up and talk to him on your level. I know you don't want to sell it anywhere else because of the desire to better the southern people. But don't cower to him, let him think you would."

Captain Frank got up without eating and said he was off to the slaughter. He picked up his leather valise with one bar of gold and three fifty dollar gold pieces in it.

Captain Franklin Dunbar nervously sat in a chair in front of President Grant, Sec. Hamilton Fish, Sec. of Treasury, Benjamin Bristow, and Sec. Orville E. Babcock. Standing around the perimeter of the oval office were four army guards, one with Frank's satchel at his feet.

"Yes Sir," Frank said, "Captain Franklin Dunbar. I served as a brigade captain throughout the war. When the war ended I went to Idaho and acquired a gold mine, with no idea of it every becoming as rich as it has."

"Yes, Captain, my young Marshall told me yesterday, of your mine," Grant said," an authoritative definition to the word bonanza. He said you wished to be a beneficiary in helping the Union to overcome this devastating depression we're in."

"No Sir," Frank said, "I told him that I could show you how to overcome the depression. True, I will help financially. You have outstanding promissory notes and greenbacks, which are backed by gold, and not the gold to redeem them. Sir, if they are not redeemed soon, it will cause a national upheaval that will be unimaginable. You could offer to pay fifty cents on the dollar. That would in my estimation take care of about half of the debt. Then Sir, issue paper money in the form of greenbacks and change the "On Demand" to read "This note is a legal Tender". The greenbacks will no longer be backed by gold, but can be used by the masses as fiet currency in small denominations of say one, two, five, and ten dollar bills, payable for all debts. I'm sure your people can make the proper arrangements to get this rectified."

There was a light applause of approval from Sec. Hamilton Fish.

"I'm curious to know what's in the bag," said Grant as he motioned to the satchel by the guard's feet.

"Oh yes," Frank said, "That is a present for you, Mister President, a token of my appreciation for the audience with you."

Grant motioned for the guard to bring the satchel, and then for him to take out the contents. The guard removed the bar and the three coins. Each man looked them over with enthusiasm and the President laid them on his desk.

"I have sixty crated box's of such ingots," Frank said, "valued at one million dollars ready for shipment, with the same amount available each six months."

Frank being aware of the fact that all men present was thoroughly enthralled, continued.

"So now, Sir" Frank said, On to the plan of alleviating the depression. It is my contention that we must put the people to work producing goods to buy, sell and trade. This is where the lower south comes into play, growing tobacco, hemp for ropes which is greatly needed for the shipping industry. Then there's corn, grist mills, and sugar cane, not only for sugar, but to make syrup, a much needed and profitable commodity."

The President interrupted. "Tell me, Captain Dunbar, who's going to cut the sugar cane. You know there are no more slaves."

"Begging your pardon, Mister President," Frank said. "In Louisiana, slaves were never used to cut the sugar cane. Chain gang prisoners from Angola, the state penitentiary, with a monetary arrangement from the sugar factories have always cut the sugar cane in Louisiana."

There were a few moments of awkward silence before Captain Frank continued. "You may also wonder how the lower south can raise crops without slaves. I'll give you a quick lesson on slavery in the lower south that you probably have never been aware of. As opposed to what is known as the upper south, which comprises Maryland, Delaware, Pennsylvania, Massachusetts, Connecticut, and West Virginia, the lower south did not beat their slaves. The owners worked in the field right along beside them, and treated them with dignity. They kept their negro families intact and did not split them up by trading them. They were well treated and respected. When they were freed, there were many that did not won't to leave, they stayed and were graciously paid for their work. People always hear of slavery like it was in the upper south where slave traders shackled and beat slaves and sold them on the open market, splitting up families and treating them like cattle. Mister President, I know you still keep your African American house servants and horse tenders in Virginia. I take it that they wished to stay with you and your family when they knew they were free."

There was more silence as Frank noticed the President's eyes turn dark and cold. Frank quickly determined the fact that he best keep talking.

"Mister President Sir, Just as a quick example, I have a friend that has a horse farm near Kansas City. He helps the Union round up hosses in Wyoming, and break them for Army hosses. He has always been a Union sympathizer, even long before the War began. He kept quite a few slaves for working with his hosses, and as house servants. He is a good example of how property owners treated their slaves in the lower south. When freedom came only one slave left his farm. He was a young man that nourished the thought of fighting for the Army. He enlisted thinking it was going to be a push-over to be a soldier. None of the others wished to leave. They loved their life as it was, and didn't relish it to be changed." Frank again wiped his brow before he continued. "Back to working on the depression, once the normal produce starts hitting the market, many other smaller industries will take suit, like the leather shops, the furniture factories, the garment factories, like the people that make pots and pans, and the glass works for producing dishes of all kinds, and the canneries will open up, cannin' foods for the groceries, and then there's the bakers, the candlestick makers, and numerous, uncountable other things, leading up to the big factories opening back up, and putting people to work. Throughout all of this getting to rolling, the new fiet currency will be making it easier for people to buy and sale.

Frank was hesitant in getting into his next subject, but he knew it had to be said, regardless of the outcome. "Now Sir," he said, "This may hit a nerve, but I have to say it. "You're idea of Reconstruction stinks to high heaven. The defeated southerners, are not contumacious over the fact of losing the war. They are very willing and wishing to be patriotic to the United States, if only they were let to be. They would like to get back to work on their farms. But they are a dignified people. They must be shown a bit of respect. It is the same way with me Sir, for me to give the Union all of my money, there has to be considerations agreed on. Right now the people of the south are being controlled by Republican politicians and Freedmen for Sheriff's in every county in all the lower half of the south. The Union militia and the atrocious Rednecks are still harassing them and occasionally burning them out of the few homes that are left, even though the war ended ten years ago.

"Mister Dunbar," Grant said in a retaliatory way, "The Union Militia and the Union Redleg division are stationed in Missouri to control the outlaw group known as William Quantrill's raiders. They are a trashy bunch of people that only want to kill the Union militia."

"Mister President, I beg to differ with you Sir," Frank was a bit irate and it showed in his tone. "Captain Quantrill, along with his Lieutenant Bill Anderson, was a Confederate bushwhacker unit comprising some 150 members long before the Civil War even started. From roughly 1854 through 1858, a bloody border war called "Bleeding Kansas" raged between residents of Missouri and Kansas over pro-Union abolitionist trying to induce anti-slavery into Missouri. Guerrilla forces from Kansas, called "Jayhawkers", and Missouri, called bushwhackers engaged in attacks against each other as well as civilians. Sir, you have to realize that Missouri was a border sharing characteristic of both North and South, but 75% of the population was from the South or other border states. After the passage of the Kansas-Nebraska Act in 1854, Clay County, Missouri, then dubbed "Little Dixie" became the scene of great turmoil, as the question of whether slavery would be expanded into the neighboring Kansas Territory came to dominate public life. Numerous people from Missouri migrated to Kansas to try to influence its future. Much of the tension that led up to the Civil War centered on the violence that erupted in Kansas between pro and anti-slavery militias. No Sir, Mister President, Quantrill was not trash, he had a purpose and he carried it out. His followers still lingers in the area to take care of the people he fought for."

Captain Frank paused momentarily to let that sink in. "Now Mister President, if you wish for me to help, then these people must be given back their dignity. The Republican governors in every state must be replaced with Southerners, and you must allow them to vote in their own state representatives and county sheriffs. You must let them up so they can be good patriots and work for your own salvation. Otherwise, Mister President, my money will go to a league of Insurrectionist that will not pussyfoot around like the Red Shirts and White Shirts. Just you remember that you are in no position to fight another war with your own people. I personally like you Mister President, and I hope in all my heart that you can see the light."

Grant's eyes looked as cold as a slithering snake, as he asked. "Captain Frank, on what side did you fight in the war?"

"I was a brigade captain throughout the entire war in the Confederate army sir. I was captured with my last six standing men on the third and final day of the Gettysburg campaign, we along with others were shuffled north to a prisoner encampment where we stayed only about four weeks until the war ended. We all signed an oath of allegiance and were shown the way south.

Grant stepped back to where Sec. Orville Babcock was seated and talked low to him. He then handed the Gold bar to the secretary of treasury, Benjamin Bristow and said something to him. Grant then left the room.

Babcock called an end to the meeting and asked Captain Frank to return in two weeks from this day. Frank nervously left the Capital building and walked the short distance to the hotel wondering if he had blown it. He arrived at his room and tapped on the door. Junior opened the door, as he and Susan were in the room with La'fay. They all looked inquisitively at him as he sat down.

"I won't know nothin' for ten days," said he, looking uneasily.

"Tell us what happened darling," asked La'fay.

"I made the President extremely angry, I believe I may have blown it. He walked out of the meeting mad as a wet hen."

Chapter 21

One week had elapsed since Captain Frank had his audience with President Grant. He and the other three Dunbar's were having the noon dinner at the hotel. The past week they had seen all there was to see around the Capital and the White House. Frank was having slight anxiety attacks awaiting some word of the meetings outcome.

"Eat your dinner darling," said La'fay, "and quit worrying. All will turn out well, you'll see."

At the table next to them were four gentlemen talking politics, as was the normal thing in the National Hotel restaurant. Frank could not but overhear their loud conversation.

"I don't know what's happening George, but the President has had his cabinet in session for a full week now. There must be something mighty important happening. He's never had them together that long at one time."

"I know David, all of the reporters have been snooping around trying with no luck to get some kind of news on it."

Frank was glad to hear that bit of gossip. He knew now that something was happening, be it good or bad. But then he knew if it was bad, it would not take a full week to consummate a rejection. He felt better.

"I have a good idea," Frank said, smiling at the other three Dunbar's, "What say let's take in a show tonight? We could go to Ford's Theatre where Lincoln was assassinated. That's a place we haven't been."

They all looked at him in wonderment. "That sounds great," Susan said, "I'd love to go." La'fay and Junior acknowledged their approval. They walked by Ford's Theatre to see when the show times were and decided to go to the matinee at 3pm. They would be seeing a musical comedy entitled "On a Spring Afternoon, in the Park." They then went back to their separate rooms to take a short nap before show time. They did do exactly that. La'fay had to awaken Junior and Susan to go to the Theatre.

The show ended just at the right time for them to go back to the Hotel for supper. They all four had delightfully enjoyed the show. Susan could not keep from talking about it. It was her first play to have every seen and was thoroughly captivated by it.

During dinner, there erupted a clamor in the street with bells ringing and horns blowing. Newspaper boys were all over the place with Extra editions on sale. A boy came into the restaurant yelling "Extra, Extra, Grant has made an about-face on the Reconstruction."

"Here boy, "let me have a paper," said Frank as he reached in his pocket for change.

In huge headlines were the words "About-Face for the South."

Frank went on to read; Grant revokes Congressional Reconstruction and orders Sec. Hamilton Fish to remove all Republican officials from Governor on down in all southern states and let the southern people immediately hold elections. Starting right now, the people are free from all restrictions and will be allowed to vote in Southern state and county elections. The article went on to say that all Union militia, including the famed Redlegs shall be immediately pulled from duty in all the southern states. "I have come to this conclusion," he stated, "because it has occurred to me that the sooner the good patriotic people of the south can start planting crops, that can be traded or sold, the sooner we will start pulling out of this horrible depression." The article also stated that all farm lands recorded in each state's county land office will automatically remain in the family name. He ended with his old slogan "Let us have Peace."

There was a noisy celebration going on all over town. Frank told the others, "Let us go up to our room and do our celebrating alone." His face was beaming with a grin from ear to ear.

La'fay was so happy she was crying, more for her loving husband than for herself. Susan was crying because La'fay was. In his elation, all Junior could thank to say was "I'll get a bottle of champagne." He did however congratulate his Dad.

On the scheduled time Frank was in the Capital lobby for his second audience with President Grant. The man at the desk recognized him and called for Orville Babcock. Babcock took Frank to his office and asked politely if he had heard the news.

"Yes Sir, I've read it over and over in the paper."

"Are you pleased with all the paper said?"

"Yes Sir, I am very pleased."

"I need to get some information from you. We need to know who is in second command in your organization.

That is who we will be conducting business with in case of your demise."

"That would be my business partner and wife of 28 years. Her name is Madame La'fay Beaudeen de Dunbar, and the home address is the Grand Hotel in South Kansas City, Missouri."

She has a permanent address in a hotel?"

"Yes Sir, our apartment takes up one third of the third floor in the hotel. And yes, it is permanent."

"Mister Dunbar, would you write down your wife's name for me. I'm not sure I would get the spelling right."

"Sure," said he, He took Babcock's pad and wrote the name for him.

"Now about shipping the gold. When can you do that?"

"I will have to wire Blackfoot, then our man there will take eight days to go to Timberline where the gold will be loaded in two wagons and come back to Blackfoot to be loaded in a waiting boxcar. That's another eight days back down the mountain. Now, if you could have soldiers from Fort Hall to help transfer the box's to the rail-car, it would expedite the whole procedure immensely. Also it would be wise to have some soldiers, as guards, from there to come to Washington with the gold. If you could take care of that, I'll see to it that a Pullman car will be sidetracked with the boxcar for them to ride in."

"Yes, we have taken care of that. The President said by all means use the soldiers in that respect. I will wire the Commandant at Fort Hall today to verify it."

"If you would Sir, have him to send a couple of soldiers up to Timberline with my man for security reasons. They still have renegade Indians up there that will sometime attack loners on the road to Timberline."

"Yes, Mister Dunbar, I'll certainly tell them to do that."

"Thank you Mister Babcock. I appreciate it. I will wire my man in Blackfoot today."

"What is your man's name?"

"I'm sorry Sir, I don't know who they sent to Blackfoot to await my wire. When I left I told them to station someone there, and I haven't had any contact as yet. When I send the wire today, I'll ask him to wire me back conformation, and give me his name."

"Yes, that should do it. Unless there's something else you need to know."

"I can't think of anything right now, Sir."

"Mister Dunbar, I hope all goes smoothly, and if you need to see me, my office is always welcome to you."

"Thank you Sir. Give the President my best."

"I will."

Within a few weeks, many farmers had moved onto their farms and built temporary shelter, so as to began clearing their land and checking the wells. Some had working tools, and neighbor helped neighbor to try to get in shape to begin farming. There was a definite need for livestock and farming equipment. As this word got out Captain Frank asked La'fay about them trying to help the people of Missouri get started by becoming neighborly benefactors, and supplying what they needed.

"Since we started all this," she said, "it seems probable for it to be our duty to help see it succeed. Now that the first shipment of gold has reached Washington, how do we go about getting some shipped to us?"

"I think Billy is still here," Frank said, "He said something about visiting awhile with Cole. I'll see if I can find him. Maybe he can help."

"Go around and tell Junior I need to see him," said she.

Frank went out the door and returned momentarily with Junior.

"Junior, I have a job for you," La'fay said, "I want you to ride the entire area around south Missouri and see who all needs financial help in getting their farms up and going. You know, with purchasing a mule and wagon, and plows, building a house, buying a milk cow, and so forth. And while you are at it, see about your own place, and hire some people to start clearing it and building a house. Buy all the livestock you will need. And, if possible try to find the freed people we had and hire them. You know that housing will be needed for hired workers too. And be sure your house is big and roomy."

"What are you talking about—my place?" said he.

"Where you were raised, dummy, we're certainly not going back to farming. It's yours and Susan's now. You see that the people's needs are on the up and up, and make a list of them. Tell them as long as the purchases are made in Kansas City, to charge them to Frank and La'fay Dunbar."

As time went by the farms in southern Missouri were looking good. Crops had been planted, breaking the ground and reaching for the sun, and the people were in their homes. It looked like a farmer's utopia once again. African

Americans and whites alike worked in the fields side by side. Political opponents had been campaigning for four months, with election day coming up in one more week. It stood to reason that all candidates were Democrat or Independents.

Billy Dunstan had wired Fort Hall in Blackfoot to send four soldiers with a team and wagon to Timberline and pick up a crate of ten bars of gold and a crate of coins from Forest Abernathy, and bring them back to Blackfoot. He then took the train to Blackfoot and returned to Kansas City with the gold, Captain Frank deposited the ingots in the bank and put the coins in his closet at the apartment. Billy, with an abundance of fifty dollar gold pieces, bid Frank and La'fay farewell and headed home to Alabama. He told them that Pierre had returned home to Louisiana, and the mine was running at top speed. He told them that the Commandant at Fort Hall said when Captain Frank needed another shipment made to wire him at the Fort, and by prior orders of the President, they will take care of it.

In another six days, Frank and La'fay were on a stage built on the side of the town square, overlooking the square. It was election day, and they were there with city dignitaries to speak for their choice for governor as people were going to the poles. A large crowd had gathered as one of the men finished his speech, and the man coordinating the speakers held up his hands and yelled across the crowd.

"Folks, we will now have Captain Franklin Dunbar to speak on behalf of our next governor—Governor Alvin A. Richardson—running on the conservative independent ticket—here is Captain Franklin Dunbar. Captain Frank stepped to the front of the stage and held his hands up high to quiet the crowd. As they quieted down there was a pronounceable "thud" followed by the crack of a rifle from across the town square. Captain Frank fell backward to the stage floor—dead.

La'fay cradled him to her bosom rocking to and fro, screaming and crying. Junior and Susan, seated in chairs behind the stage, rushed onto the stage to comfort La'fay.

Six days later Franklin Dunbar senior was buried in the Excelsior Springs cemetery some fifteen miles from where he had spent the happiest days of his life with his wife and son. More people attended his funeral than any funeral ever in Excelsior Springs.

La'fay spent the next two months in seclusion in her apartment at the Grand Hotel, with light meals served in. Junior and Susan were watching their new home being built, and picking out furniture. When La'fay began to move about, she visited Maria and Esau, Junior and Susan, and Mrs. Zerelda and Dr. Samual. While at Junior's, she asked them when she could expect her first grandchild.

"Were working fiercely on it," said Susan.

"Well try harder, I want a grandbaby to come spend some time with once in awhile."

"Aren't you going to live with us?" asked Junior.

"No son, this is Susan's home, I'll only visit occasionally. Y'all will have enough to do without me being underfoot, so I'll be staying at the apartment. You'll be seeing me regular enough. Your crops are sure looking good, and I love your home. You know, it pleases me greatly, for y'all's sake, to know that your Dad fulfilled his dream."

"Yes Mom, he'll always be remembered for that."

It had been determined by the autopsy that Captain Frank had been shot with a ball determinate with a Sharp's rifle, from an upstairs window some 150 yards across the square. The assailant was never found, and there were no known enemy's of Frank's in which to question.

EPILOGUE

The Clandestine League of Rebel Insurrectionist had successfully accomplished the dream of Captain Franklin Dunbar to institute the re-birth of the lower southern states, and return the administrative powers to the southern people. President Grant's cabinet took five days to convince him that Captain Frank's "scheme" as the President called it, was the only salvation to save the country from certain financial default and bankruptcy. Captain Frank's plan sounded to the cabinet like a godsend of prosperity, what with his ideas of bringing the devastating depression under control.

As time went by, the first year's crops were not a sufficient headway in ending the depression, but it was a start. President Grant was not nominated for a third term in office. The nomination went to James A. Garfield who won the Presidency. When his tenure ended, Grant, with his wife, embarked on a two year world tour. They first went to Briton and Ireland, dined with Queen Victoria at Windsor Castle, and with Prince Bismarck in Germany, met Pope Leo XIII at the Vatican then ventured east to Russia, Egypt, the Holy Land, Siam (Thailand), Burma, and China.

Returning to the United States, Grant and his family were left destitute. Deep in debt, he wrote a series of literary works that improved his reputation and eventually brought him out of bankruptcy. Samuel Clements offered Grant a generous contract for his memoirs, including 75% of the book's sales as royalties. Congress restored Grant to General of the Army with full retirement pay. Terminally ill, Grant finished his memoir just a few days before his death. The memoirs sold over 300,000 copies, earning the Grant family over $450,000. The Mark Twain Company promoted the book as "the most remarkable work of its kind since the *Commentaries* of Julius Caesar."

Ulysses S. Grant died on Thursday, July 23.1885, at the age of 63 in Mount McGregor, Saratoga County, New York. Grant's body lies in New York City's Riverside Park, beside that of his wife, in Grant's Tomb, the largest mausoleum in North America. Grant is honored by the Ulysses S. Grant Memorial at the base of Capitol Hill in Washington D.C.

On arriving home, Cole Younger had wasted no time in reverting to outlawry with the James brothers. After the ill-fated raid on the Northfield, Minnesota bank in 1876, Cole Younger was sentenced to the Stillwater prison, where he underwent numerous surgeries to remove eleven bullets from his body. One of the bullets had entered under his jaw and lodged just under his right eye. After one year of recuperation and rehabilitation in the prison hospital he was pardoned by an arbitrational intervention brought on by the prominent businessmen whom he had the lives spared by Quantrill during the carnage in Lawrence, Kansas.

Some years later in 1903, Cole Younger and Frank James lectured the south in their own Wild West Show. In

1912, Cole declared that he had become a Christian and repented of his criminal past. He died March 21, 1916, in his hometown of Lee's Summit, Missouri, and is buried in the Lee Summit Historical Cemetery.

Frank James suffering daily from "consumption", a disease which later was determined to be "Tuberculosis", caused him to take up a quiet life on an Oklahoma ranch shortly after Jesse was slain in 1882. Bereft of Jesse, Frank surrendered to the law and stood trial on a number of occasions and at several places. In all his trials he was defended by excellent counsel. He displayed no outward fear and always went patiently through the court procedures. Frank rode in a daycoach with a crew of Deputy Sheriff's and Major John Edwards, his friend, from one trial to another and then a third, was parades of triumph, though sick and wasted as he was, he did not care.

After numerous acquittals the state of Minnesota deemed it wiser to let well enough alone, rather than try Frank for his supposed participation in the Northfield affair. The state reversed their request for trial and stated they had no further interest in him. With no more evidence than hearsay, it would have been impossible to convict him.

Thus Frank was a free man. He teamed with Cole Younger to become a slightly hammy actor in a Buffalo Bill type of traveling tent show. When he was not earning an honest dollar as a showman, he spent his time quietly with Annie at the family home near Kearney, Missouri, or on his ranch near Fletcher, Oklahoma.

This ranch of Frank's which he called a farm, was a favorite visiting place of his mother, Mrs. Zerelda James Samuel. On February 10, 1911 after a visit, she boarded a train to return to her home in Kearney, and was stricken

195

with a collapsing heart in route and died in Oklahoma City after being taken off the train. Her husband, Dr. Ruben Samuel had preceded her in death by only three years.

In 1915, thirty-three years after Jesse's death, Frank died. After that his wife, Annie Ralston James, was never again seen in public. She died at Excelsior Springs, Missouri, on July 6, 1944, at the age of 91.

Jesse James had been shot and killed by Robert Ford on April 3, 1882. Zerelda (Zee) Amanda Mimms James, the first cousin and wife of Jesse James died November 13, 1900, in Kansas City, Missouri. She was buried at Mount Olive Cemetary in Kearney. Eighteen months after her death, her husband's body was moved from the James family farm to rest next to hers.

Jesse Edward James, more commonly known as Tim Edwards was the only surviving son of Jesse and Zee James. He and his wife Stella Francis McGowan, moved to Los Angeles, California, where he passed the Bar exam and opened a law practice. They had four daughters.

La'fay Beaudeen de Dunbar had continued to be a benefactress, spreading her wealth into Kansas City's small businesses that she deemed worthy of pursuing her husband's dream. She divided her weeks between visiting Maria and her family, and visiting Junior and Susan—and yes, their children. First was Frank Dunbar III, and then two girls, Susan Lucielle, "Lucy", and Susan Miserere "Missy". All three children had yellow hair and blue eyes. Every two weeks La'fay spent the biggest part of two days with them. She would first drive her carriage to the cemetery and put fresh flowers on Captain Frank's grave, She would sit and talk to him for awhile before she went on to Junior's house to visit with he and Susan, and her adorable grandchildren.

Billy Dunstan had become overseer for his own cotton plantation in Alabama, and was also elected as County Sheriff. Pierre Beauregard went back to Louisiana well healed, bought a big home and married his widowed high school sweetheart. He went back to work for awhile at the newly opened New Orleans mint, where in 1880, he designed and engraved the stamp-heads for the famed 1899-O Morgan silver dollar. The New Orleans Mint's coins can be identified by the "O" mint mark found on the reverse of its coinage.

In the interim, La'fay, after going to bed at night, had a habit of talking to Frank. She would keep him abreast of the daily news and happenings.

"I watched the grandkids running and playing in their yard today. I wish you could see them running and yelping like wild Indians. I also told them another story about their grandpa today."

She thought she could hear him say—*"That sounds great Baby-Doll."*

Then she cries herself to sleep—not from grief—but precious memories.

The End

About The Author

JIM FEAZELL Retired filmmaker and singer/songwriter worked in Hollywood for 22 years as a motion picture western stunt actor and cinematographer, and also performed in folk clubs and coffee houses as a folk singer.

After retiring from 17 years of stunt work he headed his own company for fifteen years in Hollywood, Ca. El Dorado, Ar. and Tucson, Az. As a member of Writers Guild of America West, he wrote and sold numerous highly acclaimed screenplays, ie; A Deadly Obsession, Two Guns to Timberline, Redneck Mama, and others. Jim wrote, produced and directed the theatrical cult movie, Wheeler, aka Psycho from Texas.

In his twilight years, Jim has become a novelist. This book "The Last Revolt" is his tenth book.

Jim Feazell Books

"feathers"
An Autobiography

An autobiography is a book about the life of a person, written by that person. Biographers generally rely on a wide variety of documents and viewpoints, an autobiography, however, may be based entirely on the writers memory. Closely associated with autobiography (and sometimes difficult to precisely distinguish from it) is the form of memoir.

I have soared with eagles ------
Here are some feathers I found

ISBN# 9781462058044 6X9 softcover $17.95
9781462058051 E – Book $ 3.99
****

Available from www.iuniverse.com via; Jim Feazell Books, Amazon, Barnes & Noble and most other book sellers.

Save money – down load the e-book to your kindle.

ESAU JONES
Bounty hunter
An Irregular Love Story

In the spring of 1865, the war had ended, the president had been assassinated, reconstruction had began before the war ended and the border country of north and south was in a state of chaotic turmoil.

Factions from both sides of the war had their lives up-heaved and destroyed beyond repair. Esau Jones was one of such men. He was only a teen age boy when he rode as a renegade bushwhacker with William Quantrill causing havoc with Union sympathizers and Union troops. During these tumultuous times, guerrilla warfare still gripped the border country of Kansas and Missouri. Bitter conflicts ensued, bringing an escalating cycle of atrocities by both sides.

As guerrilla warfare decreased more and more, ex-guerrilla's turned to outlawry for a living. Esau's friend, Jesse James, tried to get him to join him in banditry. Esau refused saying he wished to go west and find honest employment.

Through a turn of fate Esau fell into the occupation of bounty hunting. His reputation spread like wildfire among the outlaw element as the most feared bounty hunter of all time. Just to hear his name would cause one to quake in fear.

Isbn# 9781462015481 6X9 softcover $14.95
9781462015474 e book $ 9.99

Jesse
A Supernatural Thriller

Jesse's turn to crime after the end of the Civil War helped cement his place in American history as a simple but remarkably effective bandit. Displaced by reconstruction, the antebellum political leadership mythologized Jesse's exploits. During the time before and after his death, he became the subject of dime novels, which set him up as preindustrial models of resistance. During the populist and progressive eras, was when Jesse became a symbol as America's Robin Hood, standing up against corporate syndicates in defense of the small farmer. Portrayals in the 1950's pictured Jesse as a psychologically troubled individual rather than a social rebel. Some filmmakers portrayed the former outlaw as being vindictive, replacing social with exclusively personal motives. It was only shortly after Jesse's death, that in his afterlife, he began to discover ways to effectuate his desire for vengeance. Revenge on those who betrayed him. Revenge on those who sought his death.—What price could one put on a Mother's arm?—a little brother's life?—A wife's suffering? Yes—and on his own life!!

Isbn# 9781450294812 6X9 softcover $16.95

9781450294829 e book $ 9.99

Come the Swine
A Supernatural Thriller

1898 – The men of Heaven, Arkansas, committed a lunacy so evil, it opened a gate for a demon from hell. The demon established its Kingdom in the vast swamp bottom to the north of town and commanded the wild Swine to host the spirits of the dead. The evil that permeated the swamp touched the hearts of the townspeople like a contagious disease. For eighty-seven years the town grew—and the wanton immorality, larcenous and covetousness grew with it.

1985 – Chuck Abbott, an aspiring young film actor, went to Heaven in search of his missing Grandfather and entered a world of immoral and licentious inhabitants, controlled by an ARTISAN OF SATAN

Isbn #
9781462006755 6X9 softcover $14.95
9781466200038 e book $ 9.99

RETURN TO HEAVEN
A Supernatural Thriller
Sequel to Come The Swine

ISBN #
9781440176616 5X8 softcover $14.95
9781440176623 e book $ 6.00

DRY HEAT
A Police Drama

ISBN #
9780595525638 5X8 softcover $14.95
9780595525175 e book $ 6.00

THE LORD'S SHARE
A LOVE TO KILL FOR

ISBN #
7980595527625 5X8 softcover $12.95
7980595628155 e book $ 6.00

The Legend of Cat Mountain
Dual Novelettes

The Trouble With Rodney
Supernatural Mysteries

ISBN #
1971440112553 5X8 softcover $12.95
1971440112560 e book $ 6.00

MAMA'S PLACE
An Irregular Thriller
(A Redneck Chronicle)

REDNECK

A cultured intellectual and philosophical euridite.

WARNING:

If you are offended by crude, obscene, vulgar and downright sinful language. DO NOT read this book.

ISBN #
9781440189067 5X8 softcover $14.95
9781440189074 e book $ 6.00

On the Internet, pull up **Jim Feazell Books**, to review the preceding books. Thanks for your support and good reading.